Katy smiled

out to put he

Electricity shot u
into jerking her h
reaction, she asked hastily, "Is there any
chance the army would let you live if they
found out who you were?"

He shook his head sharply. "Not a chance. They have to kill me to solidify their hold on power. As long as I'm alive, the loyalists will continue to fight." He shrugged, causing all those gorgeous muscles to ripple across his chest. "The first battle may be finished, but the war is far from over."

Lovely. And here she was smack-dab in the middle of it.

She jumped when he grabbed her hand and held it tightly. For just a second desperation glistened in his eyes, then he let go of her fingers reluctantly, like a drowning man slipping into the abyss.

"Please, Katy. Help me."

Available in November 2007 from Mills & Boon® Intrigue

Forbidden Territory
by Paula Graves

Closer Encounters
by Merline Lovelace

Operation: Midnight Guardian
by Linda Castillo

Juliet's Law
by Ruth Wind

Covert Makeover
by Mallory Kane

Dark Revelations
by Lorna Tedder

The Lost Prince
by Cindy Dees

Spin Control
by Kate Donovan

The Lost Prince

CINDY DEES

First published in Great Britain 2007
by Harlequin Mills & Boon Limited,
Eton House, 18-24 Paradise Road, Richmond, Surrey TW9 1SR

ISBN: 978 0 263 85767 2

46-1107

Harlequin Mills & Boon policy is to use papers that are natural, renewable and recyclable products and made from wood grown in sustainable forests. The logging and manufacturing processes conform to the legal environmental regulations of the country of origin.

Printed and bound in Spain
by Litografia Rosés S.A., Barcelona

CINDY DEES

started flying planes while sitting on her dad's lap at the age of three and got a pilot's licence before she got a driver's licence. At age fifteen she dropped out of school and left the horse farm in Michigan where she grew up to attend the University of Michigan. After earning a degree in Russian and East European studies, she joined the US Air Force and became the youngest female pilot in the history of the air force. She flew supersonic jets, VIP airlift and the C-5 Galaxy, the world's largest aeroplane. She also worked part-time gathering intelligence. During her military career, she travelled to forty countries on five continents, was detained by the KGB and East German secret police, got shot at, flew in the first Gulf War, met her husband and amassed a lifetime's worth of war stories.

Her hobbies include professional Middle Eastern dancing, Japanese gardening and medieval re-enacting. She started writing on a bet with her mother and was thrilled to win that bet with the publication of her first book in 2001. She loves to hear from readers and can be contacted at www.cindydees.com.

Prologue

When you're a king, how you die is as important as how you live.

The unexpected thought distracted Nick long enough that he almost didn't dive for cover in time. An explosion rocked him nearly off his feet, momentarily lighting the throne room's white marble floors and colonnaded walls a gaudy shade of orange.

Kaboom!

That didn't sound like another mortar. That sounded more like a shape charge in the vicinity of one of the ancient fortress's heavy wooden drawbridges.

Dying at the hands of an enraged mob of soldiers was *not* high on his list of things to do with his life, dammit. But then, neither was being a king. Yet here he was, king for barely a week and about to die because of it. *How ironic.* Oh, he'd known his father was ill. But he'd still been shocked when the call came to his London flat that his father had succumbed to one last massive heart attack, leaving Nick sole heir to all his family's titles and estates, including the principality of Baraq.

In retrospect, his impulsive decision to stay on in Baraq after his father's funeral had been colossally stupid. But who'd have guessed he'd walk into a mess like this? What had he been thinking? It was one thing to be a fool. It was another thing entirely to die for it. Why were these guys so sure he'd be a lousy king, anyway? How could these strangers hate him so much? He'd only been on the throne a few days.

Of course, he'd just answered his own question. These Army officers kicking him off his throne were total strangers to him. He'd left Baraq with his mother when he was ten. Finished his schooling in England and only went home—although he didn't even think of Baraq as that—when he absolutely had to. The last time he'd been back here was six years ago on the fiftieth anniversary of his father becoming king.

Who would have ever guessed his perfect life would come to this? It was a hell of an end for the most eligible bachelor in all of Europe.

Flickering light danced off the ceiling, announcing that a fire blazed in the garden outside. Nick wasn't worried about the palace burning. Its stone walls were six feet thick and had withstood more than one assault by fire over the centuries.

An abrupt musical crash of breaking glass made him turn and look out from behind the massive throne. He saw several middle-aged men swing a priceless Louis XV chair and heave it out one of the room's many tall windows, creating a jagged man-sized hole amidst a glittering shower of glass.

Indignant, he stepped out from behind the throne.

Nikolas Hassan Akeem el Ramsey, thirtieth ruler of the principality of Baraq, planted his fists on his hips and glared in disgust as his ministers jumped one by one out the window into the river below. They looked like so many rats abandoning a sinking ship.

Good riddance.

They were the idiots who'd run his ailing father's country into this mess in the first place. It had taken him a matter of hours listening to their blathering and bickering to know why Baraq hovered on the edge of collapse. If only he'd had more time. Maybe he could have set the once peaceful and prosperous country to rights. But now it was too late. He was going to die a stupid, senseless death that he'd walked right into without ever getting a chance to lead Baraq into a better future.

Anger swirled through him sickeningly. Why hadn't his father seen this crisis coming and done something to avert it? *Why didn't I come home from London sooner and see it myself?*

He'd been so busy investing several large cash deposits in the Ramsey bank accounts in London, it hadn't even occurred to him to go home to visit his ailing father. Hell, he'd even passed on visiting his mother at her palatial home in Barbados this winter.

Well, he was home now.

Kareem Hadar, his father's oldest friend and only

counselor with a speck of sense, moved toward him, apparently having opted not to join the rats in their midnight swim. The older man flinched every few steps at the bursts of gunfire now echoing from within the ancient stone walls of the fortress.

"Your Highness, you must leave," Kareem urged.

Nick glared at him. That had been his exact thought moments ago, but hearing it said aloud inexplicably irritated him. "I will not! I swore at my coronation that I would stand by Baraq and defend it from its enemies."

Kareem replied urgently, "Your father is dead and this night's battle is lost. If the war is to be won, you must survive. You are the only living Ramsey."

Nick snorted. "Not for long. The rebels are inside the palace. They'll find me in a few minutes, and you know as well as I do they'll kill me on sight."

Both men ducked as a deafening blast shook the room. An enormous chandelier plunged to the floor, shattering into a million pieces and throwing a rainbow of broken crystals across the marble tiles. The huge double doors at the far end of the long hall crashed open, and a phalanx of palace guards backed into the room, hard pressed in hand-to-hand fighting. The line slowly buckled, and Nick glimpsed the distinctive green camouflage of the Army rebels pushing inexorably forward through the light-brown khaki of the Baraqi royal guards.

Resolutely he turned around and walked up the shallow steps to his father's throne. *My throne, dammit.* He pivoted deliberately and sat down. Time to die like a king.

From his excellent vantage point, he watched the

fight, mesmerized by the slow-motion collapse of the last line of defense standing between him and death. He was startled out of his reverie when Kareem grabbed his arm with surprising strength and bodily dragged him off the throne.

Nick shouted over the din, "What are you doing? If I must die, I'm going to die on my throne!"

The older man put his mouth to Nick's ear and shouted over the screams of soldiers, machine-gun fire and clash of bayonets, "Your Highness, there may be a way to avoid such a fate...."

Chapter 1

Katy McMann ached from head to foot. But then, twelve hours and counting in an airplane seat had a way of doing that. Thankfully this was the last leg of her journey from Washington, D.C. to North Africa and a postage-stamp kingdom called Baraq. Near Morocco somewhere.

She'd tried to sleep on the flight from D.C. to London, but her nerves pretty much shot that plan. This was her first mission as a humanitarian relief worker with InterAid, and she was terrified that she was going to blow it. Every newbie to the organization probably felt that way. But not every newbie lived with paparazzi camped on her doorstep, ready and waiting to catch the tiniest screwup on her part and splash it across the tabloid headlines.

It wasn't that she'd ever done anything the slightest bit newsworthy in her twenty-six years to date. But her brothers had. The McMann clan had burst onto the legal scene a few years back as the spectacularly successful lawyers to the rich and guilty. And ever since, the press had been laying in wait for them, sniffing like bloodhounds after any morsel of dirt to smear on her brothers' names—including the private life of their little sister.

The InterAid team leader, Don Ford, a marathon runner and all-around intense personality, stood up in front of the clustered team with a clipboard in hand, effectively distracting her from disparaging thoughts of her brothers and their lack of moral spine.

Ford read off a list of assignments for when they arrived in the country. She would be working on prisoner interviews with a guy named Larry Grayson. She'd met him briefly last night. He was a barrel-chested man with short, gray crew-cut hair, a fleshy face, small eyes behind wire-rimmed glasses and no lips to speak of. Rather, a white line of habitually compressed flesh marked his mouth. He'd struck her as a pompous ass who could probably quote large chunks of the Geneva Convention from memory and who took as his personal responsibility enforcing it down to the last *t* crossed and *i* dotted.

She caught a few smirks around her. Yup, she'd been stuck with Grayson intentionally. Note to self: Don Ford wasn't above putting the notorious rookie in her place. She sighed.

Prisoner interviews, eh? She pulled out her training manual and reviewed what it had to say on the subject. The job mostly involved verifying identities, ascertaining the prisoner's state of health, examining living conditions, delivering letters and care packages to prisoners and making sure no illegal interrogation methods were being employed. None of it sounded too hard.

A flight attendant came around to collect the last trash and check that everyone's seats and trays were in their upright and locked positions. Katy's ears popped gently as the plane began its descent into Baraq. She looked out the window at the barren mountains below, brick red beneath a beige layer of haze. A few pockets of green dotted the rocky landscape, but for the most part the forbidding terrain looked startlingly like Mars. And human beings lived in that? Ugh.

The plane planted itself hard on terra firma at Baraq International Airport and taxied up to a modern glass-and-chrome terminal. The ramp was conspicuously deserted. Theirs was the only plane visible on the entire field, in fact. Not exactly a teeming metropolis of activity. Of course, a coup d'état no doubt put a severe cramp on travel-related activity.

A commotion outside caught Katy's attention. She leaned forward to look out her window and saw a line of soldiers run up, surrounding the airplane. They all had machine guns at the ready, pointed at the plane. *Whoa. Dorothy, we're not in Kansas anymore.*

What sort of idiot escaped an enemy by putting himself into that very enemy's hands? An idiot with no other options, apparently. Kareem's plan was audacious. Certainly unexpected. Arguably insane. Doomed to failure. And here Nick was, going along with it like a lamb to the slaughter. Even his natural optimism was stretched to the breaking point on this one. For the first time in his life his family's money, power, prestige and sheer fame weren't going to buy him out of this mess. He was utterly without defenses or resources other than his own brains and guts. Lord, he felt naked.

Nick hitched up his bloodied khaki pants and took the machine gun Kareem handed him. "Okay. Let's do it."

The advisor nodded solemnly and started to move forward but then froze, looking over Nick's shoulder. Nick registered some sort of commotion behind him. Not good. Their plan wasn't in place yet. He opened his mouth to urge Kareem to hurry.

He never saw the blow coming. One moment he was looking into the eyes of his father's friend and the next pain exploded in his head like a starburst. The marble floor rushed up to slam into him, and then his world went black.

Their plane sat on the ramp with no one entering or leaving it for long enough that Katy finally dozed off. How long she slept, she didn't know. But it was morning when she woke up to the sounds of a commotion. A portable staircase had arrived and the front door of the jet had just opened.

A scowling soldier boarded the aircraft as if he owned it. "Everybody out!" he shouted.

The team disembarked onto the tarmac while machine guns followed their every movement. Surely this wasn't a typical welcome for relief agencies! She glanced around, and even the team's veterans had their shoulders up around their ears and looked tense. Not good.

They were herded down the stairs and into a tight group, with soldiers pressing in on them from all sides with those darned weapons. Katy didn't know about anybody else, but she was intimidated.

And then they stood there and waited some more. The tension built like a Beethoven symphony, rising higher and higher until she felt as if it might explode any second. If her brothers had been here orchestrating this confrontation, she'd accuse them of intentionally creating a crisis atmosphere in order to throw their opponents off balance.

Something incongruous struck her as she stood there. The smell of orange blossoms. It hung in the air, light and sweet, perfuming every breath she drew. And then something else struck her. The blinding blue of the sky overhead. This was actually a lovely little corner of the world. The sun already shone with an equatorial intensity that promised to burn her fair skin when it got a little higher in the sky. She sincerely hoped she lived long enough for that to be a problem.

When the standoff had reached the breaking point, a Baraqi Army officer strolled out to the tarmac and perused them scornfully. In Arabic he gave his troops a short order to stand down. At least that's what Katy, with her rusty college grasp of that tongue, thought he said.

The machine guns finally rose up and away. Along with the whole InterAid team, she sighed in profound relief.

The officer snapped at them to get their bags. She filed over to the British Airways jet and duly took her place in the bag brigade that passed their gear from the belly of the plane to the big pile of suitcases beyond the wing.

A large, heavy-duty Army truck drove up. It could've pulled up right beside the luggage, but no. It parked far enough away to make them carry their gear over to it. Clearly the Baraqi Army wasn't thrilled to have InterAid here. Katy hefted her duffel bag, carried it to the open-bed truck and tossed it up to the team member standing there.

She fell into the line of InterAid workers headed for another truck, this one sporting wooden benches along its wood-slatted sides. She was about to climb up into the transport when a heavy hand landed on her shoulder, startling her.

"You do not go with men," a soldier growled behind her in heavily accented English.

Now what? Was this more random harassment? Or maybe these guys had heard of her brothers, too? Sheesh.

"Over there." The man nodded at a smaller truck with canvas sides and roof. Her internal alarm system jangled wildly at the idea of being separated from the rest of the team. But it wasn't as though the rough hand crushing her shoulder gave her any choice in the matter. The soldier propelled her toward the enclosed truck.

She caught sight of Phyllis Estevaz, one of the team's other females, already seated inside the truck, wearing a head scarf and a shapeless black dress of some kind. Aah. An *abaya.* The black, concealing overgarment worn by women throughout the Middle East. Her guidebook had said that although the majority of the Baraqi population was Muslim, there was no official state religion in the secularly governed principality. None of the pictures of this region had indicated that women were expected to wear traditional garb.

Another soldier emerged from the far side of the truck and shoved a wad of black fabric at her. "Cover body."

She could swear he muttered the word for *harlot* in French as she took the pile of cloth from him. It smelled of sweat and dust and smoke and maybe a hint of some cooking spice she couldn't identify. She held up the *abaya,* turning it in several different directions, trying to make sense of its voluminous folds.

A female voice from behind her startled her. Hazel Whittaker, the team's third female member. "Find the neck hole and put it over your head. The opening goes in the front and ties shut. Once you've got it on, I'll show you how to put on the *hijab*—the head scarf and veil—so they don't drive you crazy."

In no time, Katy was swathed in what turned out to be some sort of polyester georgette fabric. It actually wasn't nearly as hot or uncomfortable as she'd expected. It looked like an oversize choir gown, with long loose sleeves and a baggy fit over her clothes. However, it was a royal pain in the rear trying to climb up the narrow metal steps into the back of the truck with it swirling around her legs. She collected the fabric in big handfuls, hiking it up as far as she could, but still she couldn't see her feet. A soldier snarled something at her in Arabic. As best as she could tell, he was growling at her for showing too much of her ankles. Something about being a lewd American. Tough. He could just look away if her ankles were so offensive. She had no intention of breaking her neck on these stupid steps.

The interior of the truck was airless and close. Were it not a cool, pleasant day outside, it would have been sweltering. Katy looked over enviously at the men in their open truck.

The caravan of trucks set out. They drove for nearly two hours up into the mountains, where people still lived as if it were the twelfth century. The one constant of the trip was that every woman she spied looked scared.

Finally square white-stucco structures began to cluster more and more closely together. They were coming into a large city. It must be Akuba. The capital of Baraq. Seat of the Ramsey dynasty for a thousand years, according to Katy's guidebook.

The streets were narrow and crowded. Nasal shouts of Arabic mingled with car horns. Turbaned men, young and old, stared suspiciously at them as the trucks rolled by. Women peeked fearfully from shadowed doorways, and Katy caught occasional glimpses past them into gated courtyards with colorful mosaic paving and dancing fountains. Heavily carved wood decorated the shop fronts, and a dusty smell of cumin hung in the air. She identified cinnamon and allspice, pepper and a hint of the rare and expensive spice saffron seasoning the smoke rising from pots over open-air cooking fires.

The truck turned a corner, and she caught her first glimpse of the royal palace, called Il Leone, towering over the city on its nearby mountain peak. It was an imposing pile of gray granite perched over Akuba like a hulking sentinel. Its walls were high and thick, topped by crenellated teeth of stone. A huge drawbridge was pulled shut, a medieval iron portcullis crisscrossing in front of it.

Circular towers rose up from each corner of the fortress, and striped red, black and green flags fluttered above them. The Baraqi flag pictured in her guidebook was white with the crossed swords and lions of the

Ramsey family crest emblazoned upon it. She assumed what hung now were improvised flags from the Army regime that currently held the country.

As their trucks wound deeper into the city, the streets grew even more congested and turned to cobblestone, which was incredibly uncomfortable, even in a rubber-tired vehicle with modern shock absorbers. The medieval buildings were taller here, made of stone and crowded in closely upon them, creating deep, mysterious shadows all around. Music drifted out of an open doorway—drums and a whiny, nasal horn of some kind. Katy half expected a camel caravan carrying a sultan and his harem to overtake them any second.

She felt like a well-shaken martini by the time the trucks wound through the ancient streets up to the foot of the great fortress of Il Leone. Chains clanked, and she risked lifting the canvas side of the truck to peek at the source of the noise. She saw a gigantic drawbridge ponderously folding down to admit them to the palace, its chains unwinding from great spools on either side of the cavernous entrance. The truck lurched forward, and she watched in awe as they passed over a no-kidding, murky, water-filled moat and drove into a palace courtyard. The place teemed with soldiers, and she quickly dropped the canvas flap lest she get chewed out for indecorous peeking or some such dire crime.

A soldier's face appeared abruptly at the back of the truck. In Arabic he ordered her and the other women to get out. These Baraqis were certainly not long on courtesy. Fearing a broken neck, she groped blindly for the steps with her feet and climbed down out of the truck wielding great armfuls of black fabric.

The castle walls rose around her, dark and ancient, with tiny leaded-glass windows here and there, the only relief to the stone facades. No wonder Nikolas Ramsey had preferred to run around on the French Riviera and party in London's wild and wacky West End rather than stay home and learn how to be king—if the tabloids were accurate. This place was depressing her, and she'd been here less than two minutes. Of course, he'd paid for shirking his duty in blood. And in the loss of his country.

An Army officer strode up to the InterAid team and said arrogantly in excellent French, "I am Major Moubayed. You will begin cataloging the prisoners and casualties immediately and report to me the names of every one of them." His sharp condescension reminded her of her brother Travis when a reporter was being a moron around him.

The team leader stepped forward and replied evenly, "I am Don Ford, and we will proceed according to international protocol. In due time we will, indeed, give you a complete list of casualties from both sides of the conflict, in addition to notifying the families of said casualties. We will also interview all of your prisoners and wounded to ascertain their status and treatment within the Geneva Conventions."

The major scowled, his black eyes narrow and menacing. Ford stared right back at the guy. *Patience, Don. Patience,* Katy urged silently. Finally the Baraqi officer looked away. *Nicely done, Don.*

The major growled, "Do your work quickly and be gone with you, then."

Ford nodded pleasantly and turned to face his team. "You heard the man. Let's get to work. We still have a couple hours of daylight left."

Larry Grayson materialized beside her and shoved a leather satchel into her surprised hands. "Med kit," he announced. "We're allowed to render minor first aid. Clipboard, paper and pens are in there, too, along with a spreadsheet I worked up for recording vital stats on each prisoner." She had to give the guy credit—he was organized.

"Come with me," he threw over his shoulder as he strode forward and approached Major Moubayed.

Katy hurried to catch up with her partner and reached him just in time to hear him tell the major imperiously in English, "Show me to your prisoners."

She flinched. Not the best way to handle a pissed-off authority figure like Moubayed. Sure enough, the major scowled and threw a spate of angry French at Grayson.

"Do you understand what this guy's saying?" Larry asked her, thinly veiled contempt in his voice.

She cleared her throat and said delicately, "Let's just say he's commenting on the state of American etiquette." She'd swear the Army major understood what she said, because she was sure a ghost of a grin flickered across his face.

She spoke hesitantly to Moubayed in French, being sure to look down at his shoes all the while. "Please forgive my colleague for his abruptness. He is eager to get started on the work you have requested of us.

Perhaps one of your men can show us the way to any prisoners you might be holding here?"

Apparently mollified by her humble attitude, the major signaled to a soldier, who stepped forward silently. Moubayed told the guy to take them to…someplace…a quickly uttered Arabic word she didn't recognize. The soldier nodded briskly and gestured them to follow him.

The soldier stopped in front of a bulky wooden door with a curved top, banded by iron hinges and set low in the base of a round stone tower. It looked like something straight out of the Dark Ages.

"What is this place?" she tried in French to the soldier.

"Le cachot," he replied. *The dungeon.*

Get out! A real, live, honest-to-goodness dungeon? This country was like some sort of weird time warp. She took a deep breath. Here went nothing. Her first mission as a relief worker.

The reality of standing in a tiny country halfway around the world from home, about to visit actual prisoners of war, hit her. Dauntingly. The scowling soldier beside her, casually toting a machine gun, was a whole different ball of wax than the smiling and grateful faces of hungry children she'd envisioned when she signed up for this job. A creeping sense of being an impostor stole over her. Maybe she *was* just a spoiled little rich girl playing at being a social activist, assuaging her conscience over the advantages life had granted her.

"Come on, girl!" Larry snapped. "You don't want to make these guys mad, especially since you're a female."

Like he was anyone to talk. She jumped and followed her partner hastily. Her black *abaya* flapped around her like an unruly sail, and she batted at the billowing fabric. How did Muslim women function in these stupid things, anyway? And she couldn't see squat out the veil swathing her head and covering most of her face. No wonder women weren't allowed to drive in this part of the world! In these getups they were half-blind.

She and Larry followed their escort into a round room with a desk and a couple chairs, all occupied by lounging soldiers. Their escort stepped across the space to another iron-studded door and knocked on it. A peephole slid open. Fluid words of Arabic were exchanged, and the door squeaked open ponderously. She followed Larry inside. A second soldier fell in behind them.

The sense of walking into a time warp intensified.

The passageway stretching away into blackness before them was dark and dank, lit only by torches in iron sconces on the walls. Straw littered the stone floors, and shiny black water dripped down the rock walls, its noise the only sound interrupting the heavy silence. The hallway looked carved out of the bowels of the earth itself. Katy swore she saw a rodent of some kind scurry off into the dark. Huge ancient padlocks adorned rows of ironbound doors that wound away into the gloom. An otherworldly chill skittered down her spine. This was the kind of place that touched souls. Changed them. Crushed them.

Larry glanced over his shoulder at her, grinning. "Some cool dungeon, huh? You take the doors on the right and I'll take the doors on the left. It'll go faster that way. Holler if you run into an injury you can't handle. I'm a trained trauma first responder."

"Uh, okay," Katy mumbled. She had to go solo right from the start? She gulped. This would be just like her work at the homeless shelter back in Washington, D.C., where she took care of minor bumps and bruises and lent a sympathetic ear as needed. The only difference here was that she was dressed like a mummy and standing in a medieval den of torture.

The first soldier peeled off with Larry, and the second guard went with her. She gestured at the first door, and the guy unlocked it.

She stepped forward, but the guard blocked her way. "Infidel bitch," he snarled. "Do not pollute a son of God with your filth."

She blinked, startled. Now what was that supposed to mean? That she wasn't supposed to recruit the prisoner to become Christian? Or she wasn't supposed to touch him, maybe? But she had to touch these guys to treat any injuries they might have. Crud. She'd just have to brazen it out. She had a job to do, and if this solider didn't like it, he could just lump it.

She stepped around the guard and into the tiny cell. And then she turned and shut the door in the guard's face. She took deep satisfaction from the look of surprise she glimpsed right before she all but whacked him in the nose.

Alone. Thank God. The prisoner—part of the house guard of Il Leone, judging by his khaki uniform—had a minor concussion and some minor blunt-injury trauma. She wrote down his name on Larry's spreadsheet and took note of his injuries, describing them in detail. Nothing to write home about.

At the second door, her soldier escort drew a breath to say something to her again, but she held up a hand, surprising him into silence. In resolute French she told him, "I would appreciate it if you didn't tell me how to do my job." To soften her words, she added, "And in return, I will not tell you how to do yours."

He seemed so offended by the idea of her even suggesting what he do, that he appeared unable to come up with a snappy comeback. She slipped into the second cell alone. This prisoner had a broken finger that needed splinting.

Apparently she'd achieved a hostile but silent truce with her escort guard, for he merely opened doors for her now—still glaring at her, of course, lest she think she'd won. By the fifth prisoner or so, her nerves calmed down and she fell into a groove of treating minor injuries while the men babbled out their fears, mostly over dying at the hands of their Baraqi Army captors. She couldn't blame them for the sentiment.

And then she stood in front of the sixth cell. Her escort unlocked the door and stepped aside while she entered. The padlock clicked shut behind her.

The hairs on the back of her neck prickled as she squinted into the semidarkness. The small cell was just like all the others, a ten-foot-by-ten-foot cube carved out of stone. The single tiny window high on the back wall must open onto some sort of air shaft, for indirect light filtered through it. A bucket of drinking water stood in one corner, and another bucket in the opposite corner served as a restroom facility, from the smell of it. She made out the shape of a man lying on the hip-high stone ledge that passed for a bed. He looked asleep.

The torch in her hand guttered as a cool finger of air whisked down her spine. Premonition roared through her, nearly knocking her off her feet. *This prisoner is different.*

Chapter 2

He looked much the same as the others, dirty and exhausted, wearing the beige uniform of a soldier from the royal guard. As her eyes adjusted fully to the gloom, she saw his face was badly battered and swollen. Black eyes, a gashed and broken nose, a split lip and a bad cut on the jaw were all in need of attention. Honestly his face looked like hamburger. A swollen, painful hamburger.

She spoke softly in French so she wouldn't startle him out of his sleep. *"Bonjour, je suis avec InterAid. Je suis ici pour vous aider." Hello, I'm with InterAid. I'm here to help you.*

The man's eyes flew open—as much as two puffy slits could open—staring at her, alert and wary. No panic hovered close to the surface in this guy's steady gaze. If anything, fury swirled in them. Great. Another chauvinist who felt her breathing the same air as him was an affront to his manhood.

Still, the instinctive sense of pull in her gut toward this man was unmistakable.

Shock rendered Nick speechless. Merciful God. She was gaping at him as if she *recognized* him. She couldn't. She mustn't!

He was supposed to pass himself off as a common soldier. Nobody was supposed to find out who he was. Kareem had broken Nick's nose and blackened his eyes himself and had assured him when he came to that he didn't look one bit like a king.

"Êtes vous Américaine?" Are you American, he asked. Although, how could those big, round cornflower-blue eyes in a tiny patch of lightly tanned skin revealed by her veil be anything but American?

She nodded. *"Oui."*

He switched into English, a language his guards were much less likely to know than French, and asked low and urgently, "How did InterAid get into Baraq?"

The woman shrugged. "That's way above my pay grade to know. As far as I know, we were invited."

"What are you doing here?" he demanded. Sharaf was up to no good letting these people in so soon after the coup. What was the bastard planning now?

"We're here to render humanitarian aid and monitor the treatment of prisoners."

Sharaf must be making a run at legitimizing his control of Baraq. *Dammit.* The country mustn't fall into the general's bloodthirsty hands. Chagrin at his helplessness to protect his people from the madman burned in his gut.

"Would you mind if I had a look at your nose? It could use some attention."

Nick flinched as the aid worker reached for him. She still wore a strange expression as though she half recognized him. Frantic to get her to stop looking at him like that, he stilled himself and answered smoothly, "Be my guest."

She stepped closer. The first thing he noticed was that she smelled like lavender. The scent reminded him of cottage gardens in the English countryside—enchanting and gentle. The second thing he noticed was the expression in her incredibly blue eyes. Complete disbelief about summed it up.

Either he looked a whole lot worse than he realized or she had a darn good idea of precisely who he was. Damn! He *had* to distract her. But how? His mind went completely blank. "You smell like lavender," he announced for lack of anything else intelligent to say.

She laughed as she reached for his nose. "I don't see how. I think the Army got this robe off some goat herder's wife who's never heard of bathing."

Her fingers lightly probed the swelling, and his grin turned into a grimace as shards of glass-sharp pain shot through his face. He shifted carefully and made room for her on the ledge beside him. The woman sat, her black robe billowing against his hip in a seductive slide of smooth fabric. An urge to put his hands on her, to feel the curves beneath her flowing robes, made his palms itch. He fisted his hands at his sides. *So not the time for that.* Must be some sort of primitive survival reaction kicking in because, damn, she was attractive—and all he could see of her was her eyes.

Her touch was gentle on his skin. The peroxide she used to clean his cuts stung like crazy, but he managed not to wince too much. However, when she carefully probed his broken nose again, he couldn't help but suck in a sharp breath.

She said cheerfully, "Underneath the swelling, your bones are actually aligned fairly well. You shouldn't come out of this with a crooked nose."

As if he had a prayer of living long enough for his nose to actually heal? Not bloody likely.

She asked, "Is all that blood on your shirt yours or someone else's?"

"I don't know."

"If you'll take off your shirt, I'll find out for you," she suggested.

He shrugged out of the filthy Army blouse, amused when she stared at his muscular chest. At least Kareem's hasty beating to his face hadn't cost him all his charms with the ladies.

"You're covered in blood. I'll have to wash it off to see if there are any wounds beneath it," she mumbled. There was a noticeable hitch in her voice. As if she was nervous about touching him. The idea amused him. Women he barely knew draped themselves all over him constantly as though he were their personal play toy.

He scrutinized the young woman before him, for surely she was young to react the way she did to him. She groped in her medical bag and eventually emerged with a package of antiseptic towelettes she fumbled clumsily at opening.

He leaned back against the cold stone wall and raised his arms, resting his hands on the back of his neck. His posture, suggestive of reclining in bed, seemed to fluster her even more. For some perverse reason, he was enjoying discomfiting this poor girl.

Slowly she leaned toward him. Her chest rose and fell faster under her dark robe, and her pupils dilated to black, limpid pools.

Blast him if she wasn't having the same effect on him. On full alert, he watched as she drew close. Close enough for him to see that her eyelashes were light brown. A blonde, maybe? His nostrils flared. There were only a few tiny laugh wrinkles by her eyes. Definitely young, then. Those eyes of hers were extraordinary, as clear and bright as the sky on a summer day.

Her hands settled lightly on his rib cage. They felt like an angel's kiss against his skin; featherlight, exquisitely sweet. So incongruous in this cold, hard prison.

Her gaze jerked up to meet his, surprised. For an instant, they looked directly into each other's souls. A connection leaped between them. An almost psychic knowing that went far beyond sexual awareness. Synchronicity.

Her gaze faltered, while he blinked in surprise. Who *was* this girl?

Slowly she washed him, the intimacy of the act curling around them like strands of silk, drawing them into a web that bound them inexorably to one another. Almost painfully sharp electricity shot through him at the seduction of her hands soothing his bare flesh. She petted him as she might a magnificent lion. Her touch lacked the finesse of an experienced lover, but that didn't stop it from arousing him to a stupidly feverish pitch. What the hell was wrong with him?

He supposed it had to do with her offering him solace. She didn't exactly know how to do it, but her naive sincerity made the gesture all the more appealing. He caught another tantalizing whiff of lavender and glimpsed a few strands of golden hair escaping her head scarf. An intense desire to see the face beneath the veil surged through him.

Her compassion made him want to put his arms around her and hug her in gratitude. She was a priceless reminder of the sane, normal world that existed somewhere beyond the walls of his prison. He closed his eyes in sudden pain. He hadn't realized just how isolated he felt until she had arrived.

Her fingers lightly probed his ribs, looking for broken bones. "If you'll lean forward," she murmured, "I'll check the ribs in your back."

He bent toward her, his arms coming up to surround her lightly. She jumped like a frightened doe in his arms.

"Uh, not exactly what I had in mind, but I suppose it works," she mumbled in consternation.

It felt as if he'd captured a rainbow, all light and air and fragile color. He held her delicately while a powerful protective impulse slammed into him. He couldn't recall the last time he'd reacted to a woman like this. It must have something to do with that whole business of being about to die.

He didn't go for fragile females. The women he generally ran with could take perfectly fine care of themselves, thank you very much. But then, given that this young woman was here in the middle of an ongoing war, she probably could, too.

He smiled into the folds of her veil as her hands traced the ribs in his back, checking for broken bones. Her fingers trembled against his skin. And something inside him trembled in response.

Surprise coursed through him. He didn't know which one of them was more flustered at the moment.

"Poking you like this hurts, doesn't it? I'm sorry," she breathed.

He opened his eyes and gazed down at her intently. Her eyes had tiny flecks of silver within the palette of vivid blue. "Don't be sorry," he murmured. "It's a nice change from guards pounding the hell out of me."

She met his gaze for several candid seconds. Their faces would be in kissing range were it not for the black silk covering her mouth and nose. She meant him no harm. Wanted to help him. He saw it in her eyes. The weird electricity surged anew between them.

Was it possible? Was there a chance that help might reach him from the outside? If someone like this were to be sympathetic to him, maybe pass a message to a few supporters of his in the city—

It could work.

Maybe his death wasn't so inevitable after all!

But first he would have to convince her to help him.

Alarmed at her totally inappropriate reaction to this anonymous Baraqi man, Katy slipped out of the loose circle of his arms to reach into her medical bag, relieved to be out of such proximity to the strangely attractive prisoner.

She fumbled for her clipboard and placed it squarely between them, lest he get any frisky ideas in the meantime.

"What's your full name?" she asked in as business-like a fashion as she could muster.

He didn't answer right away. She looked up, her pen poised over the right box on Larry's spreadsheet.

He was frowning at her. Intently.

She commented lightly, "It's not that hard a question. I just need to write your name down for our records. It's required by the Geneva Convention for you to give your captors your name anyway."

Still no answer.

"Are you having trouble remembering your name?"

He sighed. "I'm trying to decide whether or not I should trust you."

She slid her pen into the top of the clipboard and set the whole thing down. She said pleasantly, "Well, I've been sent here to help you. If not me, who are you going to trust?"

Another heavy sigh. "Therein lies my dilemma. You're all I've got."

Maybe it was the constant browbeating she took over her unfortunate family connections that made his comment rub her the wrong way. But she said a little less pleasantly, "I am a fully trained humanitarian relief worker and I'm generally considered to be a reasonably intelligent human being who doesn't lie, keeps her word and is classed as trustworthy."

And, unaccountably, he smiled. "Aah, there it is. A spine. Perhaps you are the person I need after all."

Huh?

"Answer me this," he continued. "Who's going to see that spreadsheet of yours?"

"My team will. General Sharaf's people will. And I expect we'll forward the list to the Red Cross."

He reached into his pocket and pulled out a vinyl-covered passport. "Then, in that case, my name is Akbar—" a pause while he read the document "—Mulwami."

She frowned. And didn't bother to write it down. That *so* wasn't his name.

He glanced up at her. "Do you need me to spell that?"

She snorted. "No. I need you to quit BSing me."

He laughed, back to his utterly charming self. "Aah, you and I are going to get along famously. I promise you that is my name as the Baraqi Army knows it to be."

"And what does your mother know it to be?" she retorted.

He leaned back against the rock wall behind him. "I'll answer that question if you wish. But first you must promise me something."

Man, his dimples were lethal. "What's that?"

"You must solemnly swear not to do or say anything that will get me killed."

Her eyebrows shot up. "Killed? Of course not. I'm here to save lives."

His voice vibrated with intensity. "Do you *swear?*"

Katy replied without hesitating, “Of course I do. It’s my job to protect your life to the best of my ability.”

He nodded slowly and murmured so quietly she had to lean close to hear him. “My friends call me Nick. But my mother calls me Nikolas.” A long pause. “Ramsey.”

Chapter 3

In a ravaged corner of Akuba, in a windowless room lit only by the flickering light of a pair of lanterns, a group convened in secret; a dozen dark-robed women, their faces hidden according to the edicts issued by General Sharaf—leader of the coup—only hours ago. Any woman who did not follow the strict religious dress code he'd declared would be whipped.

In a whisper the self-appointed leader of the group asked, "Has anyone received word whether the king is alive or dead?"

A shrug from a castle insider. "Nobody knows. He was seen sitting on his throne moments before the Army burst into the great hall. But that is the last report anyone has of him."

"Fool," the leader bit out. "Nonetheless, he must

be found. Sharaf must not be allowed to kill him. All our hopes rest with a Ramsey staying in power. Sharaf will strip away every right women have ever had under the Ramseys."

One of the others spoke hesitantly. "I heard General Nagheb phone someone he called InterAid this morning. He asked them to come monitor prisoners in Baraq. If Sharaf allows them in, perhaps we can make contact with them. Get them to assist us in searching for Nikolas Ramsey."

The leader shrugged. "Perhaps. We can try. But most of those groups choose to remain neutral. In the meantime, we must look to our own resources to find the king and extract him from the clutches of the Army. All of us must make this our one and only goal for now. Understood?"

Nods all around.

"Very well, then. Go and be safe. And remember—we *must* find the king before Sharaf does. Our futures and our daughters' futures depend on it."

The twelve women rose silently to their feet and slipped one by one out into the frightened, waiting city.

"Nikolas *Ramsey?*" Katy exclaimed.

"Good Lord, woman, keep your voice down! You just swore not to get me killed!"

"Nikolas *Ramsey?*" she repeated in a shocked whisper.

He shrugged. "In the flesh."

"What in the world are you doing here?" Although, as soon as she asked the question, the answer was obvious. He was hiding from Sharaf. But in prison? "*Why* here?"

"There was nowhere else to go. We were surrounded and the palace was overrun. It was this or die. Although, I think death is probably inevitable for me, don't you?"

He asked that last bit conversationally. As if they were talking about the weather. "Death is inevitable for all of us," Katy retorted wryly. "The question is when."

"Sooner rather than later for me, I should think," he said dryly. "As soon as my face heals enough for me to be recognized."

She examined it critically. "You're pretty messed up. Honestly you look like Quasimodo."

He looked pained for a moment, then said lightly, "Thank God for small favors."

"That won't protect you forever," she said quietly.

He met her gaze briefly and then his slid away. "No, it won't."

She got the impression he wanted to say more, but he didn't. Sympathy washed over her. What a rotten way to spend your final days—waiting and watching the clock tick until your body betrays you and your captors recognize and kill you.

She said, "If there's anything I can do to make you more comfortable, let me know. I'll see what I can do."

He laughed briefly without humor. "How about a hacksaw and a helicopter?"

She smiled gently and reached out to put her hand on his. Electricity shot up her arm, startling her into jerking her hand away. To cover up her reaction to him, she asked hastily, "Is there any chance the Army would let you live if they found out who you were?"

He shook his head sharply. "Not a chance. They have to kill me to solidify their hold on power. As long as I'm alive, Ramsey loyalists will continue to fight."

She replied, "The way I hear it, the fighting's pretty much over and the Army's in control of the country."

He shrugged, causing all those gorgeous muscles to ripple across his chest. "The first battle may be finished, but the war is far from over."

Lovely. And here she was, smack-dab in the middle of it.

She jumped when he grabbed her hand and held it tightly. "Listen. Whatever you do, you can't tell the Army who I am. They'll kill me the second they know."

"I understand." The zinging energy of the man was shooting through her again, but this time she was ready for it. "Truly. I swear they won't find out from me."

For just a second desperation glistened in his eyes. He let go of her fingers reluctantly, like a drowning man slipping into the abyss. He whispered, "Please. Help me."

She thought fast. "Tell you what. I'll look into the legalities of it. There might be something we can do. You are a head of state, after all. There might be some special rule of prisoner treatment we can invoke in your case. Tonight I'll take a look at the Geneva Conventions and see what I can find."

"Don't talk to your boss about me. Don't talk to anyone. Trust no one."

Why the heck not? Aloud she said, "InterAid is not in the business of getting anyone killed. My boss will keep your secret."

He surged to his feet, looming over her. "Swear to

me you will not tell anyone who I am. It must remain our secret. My life depends on it."

She stared up at him for several seconds. He knew something he wasn't telling her. Currents of intrigue flowed all around this place, this man. One thing she knew to be true—Nick was really worried about being double-crossed. Although that was probably part and parcel of being a prince his whole life. A rich, handsome, eligible one.

"I said I won't tell anyone and I won't."

"Thank you."

His simple words were a caress. A reverent touch gliding across her skin. And she was losing her mind. The guy was bruised and battered and filthy, and she was panting after him like a dog in a sauna.

But then he did touch her. And it was a hundred times more seductive in the flesh. His fingertips brushed the back of her hand lightly. Beseechingly. Desperately.

"Be careful. The very fact that you know who I am places you in grave jeopardy, as well."

She blinked, alarmed. "How? I'm just a random relief worker."

"This is Baraq. Nothing is simple here. There are plots within plots everywhere. Layers within layers to every plot. If I am killed, you could bear witness to the fact that I was murdered by the Army well after the coup itself was over. They can't afford to have that information become public. The Baraqi people and world opinion will not tolerate a bunch of murderers ruling this country. *That* is why they'll kill you, too."

She absorbed his words in silence. Damned if what

he said didn't make perfect sense. Foreboding clutched at her throat like a cold, bony hand.

He murmured urgently, "I'm not exaggerating. *Trust no one.* Both of our lives depend on it."

His golden gaze bored into her in uncomfortably intense entreaty. He certainly believed his warnings to her, at any rate. Should she?

He exhaled a long, slow breath and said beseechingly, "Please. My life is in your hands."

He didn't sound as though he used the word *please* often. And that was the second time he'd used it with her. Despite his breezy charm, this guy was scared stiff. And she couldn't blame him. Sharaf's men hadn't exactly made the world's friendliest first impression on her.

Saying "please" was probably a big concession for him. The guy was a king, after all. At least he'd sounded sincere when he'd said it. Maybe she was wrong to protect this guy. Maybe she should ignore his advice and tell her boss who he was after all—

His voice interrupted her troubled thoughts. "I believe you were going to put a bandage on my nose?"

"Right," she mumbled. "Bandage. The bigger, the better."

"Exactly." His relieved smile lit up the room like a floodlight. He added under his breath, "Thank you."

She got the distinct feeling she'd just stepped over some sort of invisible line. And, once crossed, there was no going back.

Katy stumbled through the rest of the day's work in a daze, mechanically treating prisoners and recording their condition on her clipboard. Alive! The king of Baraq was alive! And she was the only person who knew it. Was her life really in danger? Or was Nikolas Ramsey just trying to scare her into silence? Should she ignore his warning and tell someone of her discovery or was discretion the better part of valor? One thing he was right about: palpable currents of intrigue flowed around her as she made her way through the palace toward the exit a few hours later.

Unseen eyes glared at her, and she caught the furtive looks and snide comments the Army soldiers cast at her when they thought she wasn't looking or listening. It was one advantage of the veil over most of her face. Nobody could see her reaction to their jabs, uttered mostly in Arabic they thought she wouldn't understand. She'd studied the language for four years in college, and it was coming back to her rapidly. She got the distinct feeling her well-being might rest on her secret comprehension of the tongue. *Nope, not gonna let on that I understand them just yet.*

The Army didn't deign to provide the aid workers transportation to their hotel, so Katy, Larry and two other team members, who'd been treating the more seriously wounded prisoners housed in the palace proper, convened at the main drawbridge at dusk to walk to their lodgings. Soldiers all but pushed them out a man-sized postern gate within the larger drawbridge. The good news was the walk was steeply downhill into the crowded city streets. The bad news was the hike back up the hill tomorrow morning was going to be a bear.

When they arrived at the hotel, Katy was segregated

from the men and given a room on a floor allotted only to women. Her room was sparse and in need of a good cleaning, not to mention stuffy with the remnants of the day's warmth. There was one toilet for the entire floor of twelve rooms and *one* bathroom with an old claw-foot bathtub. At least it was clean and in good working order.

She sat down on her bed and winced at the sag in the mattress. But, hey, it was better than the stone ledges the prisoners were sleeping on. She stripped off her *abaya,* considering whether it would be dry by morning if she washed it right then. She opened her suitcase, which had magically appeared in her room. And stopped cold. Someone had searched it. The clothes weren't folded right, and her things weren't in the same places she'd put them when she'd left home.

She went next door and knocked on Hazel's door. The older woman stuck her head around the jamb. "Oh, it's you. Come on in."

Katy stepped inside and grinned at Hazel's shorts and halter top. No wonder the woman had hidden behind the door. She'd be arrested if any Baraqi Army type saw her in such lascivious garb. "Was your suitcase searched, Hazel?"

The older woman looked up at her quickly. "No. Was yours?"

For some reason, a twinge of foreboding made her reticent to tell anyone about it. Maybe it was Nikolas Ramsey's warning. Or maybe it was a gut instinct. Her brothers swore by them. She shrugged. "I guess I'm just getting paranoid after the way the Army's treating us women."

Again Hazel shot her a strange look. "They've been exceedingly polite to me and Phyllis. Did you do something to make them mad?"

Katy blinked. "Not that I know of." On yet another hunch, she asked, "Do you speak Arabic?"

Hazel nodded. "Fluent in it. I can argue politics and cuss out a cab driver with the best of them."

"And there haven't been any nasty comments or innuendos flying around you from the soldiers?"

"Nope." Hazel looked at her closely. "You going to be able to hack it in this country?"

Katy drew herself up straight. "Of course." Why in the world was she being singled out for harassment by the Army? Surely they didn't know or give a flip for who her brothers were!

The older woman nodded. Paused. Told her sagely, "Don't go out by yourself. Eat in the hotel or go with a group into the bazaar to buy food. And don't touch any of the meat from the street vendors. It'll give you a case of Montezuma's revenge you'll never forget."

Katy smiled at the small overture of friendly advice. "Thanks."

Hazel nodded briskly.

Thoughtfully Katy wandered downstairs to snag a couple pieces of fruit and returned to her own room. She unlocked the door and let herself in. Night had fallen while she'd been gone, and she had to cross her room to reach the lamp in the corner. The white gauze curtains billowed in the breeze, and again she stopped cold.

She hadn't left her window open.

She turned around slowly, scanning the dark corners

and shadows dancing in her room. Nothing there. She was alone. She let out a slow breath. Still in the dark, she moved over to the floor-to-ceiling casement windows and shut them. She made a special point of locking them, as well. Only then did she move over to the lamp and switch it on. It bathed the room in soft yellow light.

She looked around again. And froze. There was something on her pillow. *A note.* She moved over to it and looked at it without touching it. It was a single sheet of beige linen stationery folded in half. In cramped cursive were the letters *M-l-l-e,* the French abbreviation for *Mademoiselle.* Gingerly Katy picked it up. Unfolded it. More of the cramped cursive.

She translated the French quickly in her head.

> King Nikolas is not dead, and we desperately need your assistance in finding him. Please help us in this vital endeavor, *mademoiselle.* We shall wait with utmost urgency until you succeed. We will contact you soon. Be warned—there are those within the lion who would use you to gain their own ends.

Within the lion? Of course. Il Leone. The palace. So, rumors were already floating around that King Nikolas lived, were they? That didn't bode well for the man she'd met earlier. Of course, the warning in this note didn't bode well for him, either. If his enemies were already watching her, then she'd have to be extremely careful not to lead them to the hidden king.

And then there was the direct threat to her. Someone

in the palace wanted to use her for some reason, eh? Why was that just not a surprise? Who could this note be warning her of? Major Moubayed and the Army? Nikolas himself?

The more relevant question at the moment was who had gotten into her room to leave this cryptic little message? And how? She was sure the door had locked shut behind her when she'd gone next door to talk to Hazel. And there was no way she'd left the window open. She even remembered thinking the room was too warm and closed it before she went out. Surely nobody had climbed up the face of a five-story building to sneak in her window and deliver this note! Someone on the hotel staff with a master key, then?

She picked up the phone. A female operator answered in English. Now how did she know to do that? She must have a list of the room numbers the Americans were staying in. Katy asked, "May I please speak to the manager?"

"Regarding what, Miss McMann?"

Katy replied, "Someone has broken into my room. I need to report it to the manager and the police."

The operator answered without any noticeable surprise, "I will report it to the manager right away, ma'am."

That was weird. Shouldn't a break-in alarm a hotel employee at least a little bit? And the woman didn't ask if anything was stolen or if Katy was okay. Katy replied, "I really would prefer to speak to the manager myself."

"That is not possible, *mademoiselle*." The woman's voice shot up by at least half an octave, and now definite alarm rang in her tone.

Katy blinked. Had the operator just called her *made-moiselle* on purpose? She replayed the sentence in her head. That was definitely a special emphasis the woman had placed on the word. What in the world was going on here? She could understand the hotel not wanting to involve the police. Especially with the city under martial law. But why was the operator running interference on her at least speaking to the manager?

"I swear to you, *mademoiselle,* no harm will come to you in this hotel."

There it was again. That heavy emphasis on the word *mademoiselle.* And real desperation coursed through the operator's voice now.

"Uh, okay. I believe you. I will leave it in your hands to report this to the manager and the authorities."

Katy frowned through the woman's gushing thank-you. "What's your name?"

"I am Hanah."

"Thank you for your help, Hanah."

"You are welcome. And thank *you.*"

Katy hung up the phone, roundly confused. The hotel operator had left her this note? Clearly if Hanah wasn't the author, the woman was at least aware of its existence. Why would someone in the hotel feel obliged to warn her about treachery in the palace?

Speaking of which, she had some homework to do. She checked the window latch again and carefully locked the door behind her as she stepped out into the hall. Hopefully there was no law against women going to a men's floor to visit in this backward country. She made her way downstairs and knocked on Don Ford's door. He opened it immediately. A group of six men from the team were seated on the floor, a large picnic spread out on a cloth between them. It looked as if they were having a great time. A pang at being excluded stabbed her gut.

"What can I do for you, Katy?" Don asked.

"Do you have a copy of the Geneva Conventions with you?"

"Which one?"

"The one pertaining to treatment of prisoners of war," she answered.

"Do you want all one hundred and forty-three articles plus annexes or one part in particular? Did you run into a problem today?"

Again her internal alarm bells went off, shouting at her not to answer that question. "I just want to read up on a few things," she answered with what she hoped was casual ease.

"I'll get it." Ford went across the room to dig in a big leather satchel.

One of the other men looked up at her slyly. "How'd it go working with Larry?"

She smiled pleasantly and said without missing a beat, "He was an absolute dear. I'm so glad Don paired me up with him."

Everyone gawked in surprise and she bit back a grin. There. Let them chew on that. Nothing like killing 'em with kindness.

Ford held out a sheaf of papers about sixty pages thick. "There you go. Holler if you have any questions about what it means."

As if after growing up in her family she couldn't read legalese and make sense of it? She smiled politely and said smoothly, "Thanks. I'll be sure to ask if anything comes up that's beyond me."

Good ole Don blinked rapidly a couple times, as if he'd just remembered who she was. A little red around the gills, he showed her to the door and wished her good-night.

She fumbled loudly at her door for long enough to let someone climb out her window. She entered her room cautiously, gun-shy at the idea of accidentally surprising an intruder. But all was as she'd left it.

She settled on her bed to look for a loophole in the document Ford had given her. Nada. The only thing the document had to say about treatment of heads of state as prisoners was that they should be afforded quarters fitting to their station. Big freaking lot of good that would do Nikolas.

And then she ran across the bit about prisoners of war withholding their identities from their captors. Failure to identify oneself truthfully negated one's right to full protection under the Geneva Convention. Great. Nikolas could tell the Army who he was, get a great room for a night and then get killed. Or he could not tell them and be subject to abuse or even torture. He'd have to continue to be Akbar Mulwami for the time being. It was flimsy protection, but he didn't have any other options.

As for telling her boss who Nikolas was, something in her gut said the fewer people who knew Prisoner 1806's secret, the better.

While she rinsed out her *abaya,* she debated whether

or not to sleep with the window closed and opted not to let the mysterious note intimidate her into being miserable. She lay down on top of the sheets and let the evening's cool breeze waft over her, carrying that faint, lovely smell of orange blossoms again. A siren sounded in the distance, a distinctive up-down-up-down wail. A few vehicles rumbled past, rattling on the cobblestones. How a night this peaceful and quiet should follow so closely after the violence she'd seen on television just two days ago was hard to fathom. Grateful for the lack of mortars and explosions, she fell asleep.

And dreamed of a handsome prince with golden eyes carrying her off to an enchanted palace and making love to her all night long.

Nick lay on the cold stone shelf that was his bed for long hours after the American left, nurturing the tiny spark of hope she'd ignited deep within him. If he had an ally on the outside, maybe, just maybe, he might get out of this alive. And then he might get a chance to set this mess aright, to make up for everything he'd failed to do before.

But first things first. He had to get out of here. And that wasn't in the cards for him. Eventually his face would heal, the swelling would go down and then he'd be recognized. He was a dead man walking.

The problem with being locked up in a silent, dim cell like this was it gave a guy plenty of time to think. He'd spent the last two days in this black hole damning himself to hell and back for neglecting his duty for so many years. For much of his thirty-four years, he'd jetted all over the world, living as fast and playing as hard as he could, running away from the responsibilities that came with his family's wealth and position. Hell, just running away from his family.

He bitterly regretted now never having spent time with his father after college, never trying to talk to him about how he ran his country, about his vision for Baraq. Lord knew, Baraq had been his father's passion in life. To the exclusion of all else—including his wife, who'd eventually left, and his only son, whom he'd mostly ignored.

Nick knew far too little of his Ramsey legacy. But he did know he'd failed that legacy. For thirty generations—almost a thousand years—dominion over these lands had passed from father to son in an unbroken line. And he was going to break the chain. He would go down in history as the last Ramsey. The one who failed. Spectacularly. The thought galled him.

His father might have been a bad parent, but in the clarity that came with staring death in the face, he admitted to himself that he'd also been a bad son. And obviously the Army believed he was going to be a bad king or else they wouldn't have overthrown him before he could prove them wrong. Not only had he failed the Ramsey dynasty, he'd failed himself.

His remaining life span could no doubt be measured in days rather than weeks or years. Surely someone would recognize him soon. And then the Ramsey line would end.

Unless…

The idea was preposterous. The American aid worker would never go for it. It wasn't fair to ask her such a thing. He barely knew her, for goodness' sake! He had no right to put an innocent young woman's life at risk any more than he already had.

But what other choice did he have?

He couldn't sit by and watch his family disappear without a trace. He couldn't leave his countrymen with no hope at all of continuing Baraq's proud heritage, which was so closely tied to his family's. If there was even a chance of salvaging the line, he had to try.

He wrestled through the night with his misgivings, examining his idea from every angle, analyzing its chances for success, anticipating the pitfalls and planning how to get around them. And his idea was full of holes. Huge, gaping craters. Starting with the fact that it all hinged on the American woman.

But after a long, sleepless night, he finally came to a single conclusion. He had no choice. He *must* try.

Chapter 4

The worst of Katy's jet lag was gone when the first call to morning prayer broadcast across the city at dawn. She went over to her French door and, leaning on the jamb, gazed out across Akuba as sunrise bathed the white metropolis in vivid peach hues. Ox-drawn carts laden with fresh produce lumbered by on the street below, and veiled women met the carts at their front doors, bartering in quick Arabic and filling woven bags with food in a ritual as ancient as the city itself.

Gold onion turrets and the tall needles of minarets marked mosques. Tapering white steeples marked the Christian edifices on the skyline as the sun broke over the horizon and morning burst upon the city at her feet. The first shopkeepers slid back grates from the fronts of their shops and spread out blankets on the sidewalk, arranging their wares for sale. Brass and woven goods, tobacco and spices, piles of fruit, loaves of bread, small electronics and racks of CDs and DVDs emerged to line the margins of the street. The blend of old and new was oddly representative of the city itself.

With the reality of a new day came insidious doubt that she'd actually found Nikolas Ramsey yesterday. Maybe the guy just looked like the king and was hoping to parlay that into some sort of negotiated release. Time to go see if her imagination had been playing tricks on her or not. She had dozens of prisoners to see today, but somehow she'd make time to pay a return visit to him. She donned her mostly dry *abaya* and managed to get her scarf tied around her head and the veil across her face with the help of the tiny mirror in the corner of her room.

Too nervous to eat much more than a single, delicious honey cake, she hiked up the killer hill to Il Leone, and the climb sucked every bit as bad as she'd expected it to. Nobody needed stair-climbers in this town! Her *abaya* clung to her sweaty skin, and the silk veil clung to her face in the most annoying fashion when she and Larry finally staggered into the palace courtyard, huffing like racehorses. More like broken-down, asthmatic horses ready for the glue factory.

Throughout the morning a number of the prisoners asked her under their breath and with some urgency whether there'd been any word on King Nikolas. Did she know if he was alive or dead, and where? Did Nikolas, despite his playboy ways, engender loyalty in his troops? Or were they simply being questioned hard about him by the Army?

It ran against her grain to lie, but it wasn't as though she had any choice. She shrugged and told the men she hadn't heard anything and that InterAid was not supposed to get involved in such matters. *Right.*

Many of the prisoners were in bad shape. Most of their injuries could have come from the rigors of combat, but she suspected that many of them had actually come from beatings administered during their initial interrogations. The soldiers controlling the palace were rude to her and arrogant enough to set her teeth on edge. It was easy to dislike this bunch of thugs who'd taken over Baraq. They might have legitimate reasons for what they'd done, but their methods left a great deal to be desired.

Moving from prisoner to prisoner within the palace, it didn't take Katy long to figure out that the coup had been planned for some time prior to Nick's father's death. He'd died a lingering death of heart disease, apparently, and the Army had waited only for the poor man to stop breathing to seize the kingdom. Larry commented to her that the former Ramsey king had been so popular that no coup against him would have worked anyway. Not so with the younger Ramsey. Everyone she came across, both rebel and royalist, agreed that Nikolas was a complete stranger to them.

It was midafternoon before she was able to make her way back to Prisoner 1806 without it seeming unnatural. But finally she stood in front of the iron-banded door once more.

Her guard escort today was named Riki. He was a gregarious youth who swore he was eighteen, but she'd put his age at closer to fourteen. He was a distinct departure from yesterday's surly escort, and for that she was grateful.

"I'll be with this prisoner for a while," she informed the boy.

Riki shrugged and reached for the door. She waited impatiently while he fumbled with the rusty lock. Finally it creaked open and she stepped inside.

The prisoner was sitting up when she entered, one foot propped up on the ledge and his arm resting across his knee. Their gazes met and locked, their shared secret hanging heavy in the air between them like the scents of cinnamon and curry that hung over the city. She hadn't imagined a thing. It was all real. The aristocracy cloaking him, the impatience of a man used to getting his way. The sheer royalty of the man. He *was* the king.

She stepped farther into the cell. His expression was warm, an intimate caress that pierced her robes to touch her skin in the most disturbing fashion. Katy actually felt herself flush under her veil. Even in heavy gloom, wearing a ruined uniform, his face as battered as a prizefighter's, he oozed magnetism—heck, outright sex appeal. How could anybody mistake him for a common soldier? But then, maybe it took a woman to sense it. And the Baraqi Army was notably lacking in women in its ranks.

She waited for the heavy door to lock behind her before she spoke. "How are you today?"

"My nose feels much better. Thanks for the bandage."

His gaze seemed to strip the robe right off her.

Instead of feeling safely swathed in shapeless yards of cloth, she felt exposed. Naked.

"And how are *you* today?" he asked, his voice mellow and intimate.

She frowned. She could really do without this whole turn-on-the-charm thing. It was incredibly effective—and distracting. "Fine, thank you."

"Have a seat." He scooted over to make room for her on the crude ledge. "So. What did you find out about protecting my identity?"

She shook her head regretfully. "The Geneva Convention is clear. You have to tell the Army your name or else forfeit protection under the Convention."

He asked soberly, "Are you required to notify them that I no longer have Geneva Convention status?"

"It doesn't say specifically that I have to."

"So what the Army doesn't know won't hurt it. Until they figure out who I am and that I've broken the rules, I'm safe."

She glanced around at the dank stone walls and replied drily, "I'm not sure I'd call this safe."

"Hey, it's safer than flying around a Formula One race course at two hundred miles per hour."

She snorted. "Not in my book."

"Well, it's a lot safer than navigating a room full of social-climbing, money-lusting, crown-seeking women looking to trap me into marriage."

"You have a point there." Her grin faded. "How can you joke around at a time like this?"

He shrugged, an elegant movement of his broad, athletic shoulders. "How can I not? I prefer laughter over the alternative. By the way," he added casually, "if you'd like to drop your veil while you're in here with me, I won't tell on you."

Surprised by the offer, she gazed at him searchingly. Funny, but she was shy about showing him her face. Would he think she was too forward if she took off her veil? Oh, for heaven's sake. The guy'd lived in England since he was a kid! He was perfectly accustomed to western women. If anything, it must be strange to him to see women all covered by veils.

"Please," he murmured. "Give me a pretty face to think about as I languish here waiting for my luck to run out."

Was she pretty? She wasn't exactly ugly, but she'd never been overly concerned with her looks. She wore decent clothes and put on makeup when she thought a camera crew might be lurking outside her apartment, but that was about it. This man was no doubt used to looking at exotic, gorgeous supermodels.

Had she detected a hint of desperation in his lightly voiced request? She cast a glance around the medieval dungeon. He must be going crazy staring at these featureless and depressing walls in near-total darkness. It was a simple enough thing to grant the poor guy. She reached up and removed the safety pin securing the end of the veil but blinked in surprise when he brushed her hand aside and reached for the veil himself. The black silk caressed her cheek as he slowly lifted the panel of fabric aside.

Why showing this guy her face should be a big deal, she had no idea. But here she was, holding her breath like some Moorish virgin on her wedding night. Sheesh. She risked a glance up at him. A faint smile curved his lips as he regarded her like a connoisseur observing fine art.

"Lovely," he breathed. He let the silk slide from his fingers to trail down over her breasts.

She shrugged, embarrassed. "I suppose. If you go for that wholesome all-American look."

He laughed lightly. "You must remember—in this part of the world, your blond hair and blue eyes are exotic. Very few women here share your coloring." He chuckled and added, "Admittedly I've spent most of my life in England. But to my eye, most people there are one shade or another of paste-white. Your tan is a nice departure from that. And you have extraordinary bones."

Bones? Uh, okay. If he said so. He was the connoisseur, after all. And as for being exotic, she'd never thought of herself that way. Belatedly it occurred to her that if she'd been in a bar and he'd said that, she'd have blown off his observation as a pickup line.

"What's your first name, Miss McMann?" he asked.

"Katy."

"Is it just Katy or is that short for something?"

"My real name's Katrina, but I've always hated it."

"It's a beautiful name, like its owner. But if you insist, I shall call you by your so very American nickname."

Why in the hell did his blatant flattery knock her off balance like this? Aspiring young lawyers hit on her all the time, trying to get an introduction to the legendary McMann clan. And of course, there were the fortune seekers who mistakenly thought she lived off her brothers' wealth. And then there were the occasional jerks who'd hit on anything in skirts.

She mumbled, “What should I call you?”

He grinned. “Under the circumstances, we’d better stick with Prisoner 1806. Or Akbar,” he added.

She looked up, startled at the dry humor in his voice. His stunning eyes sparkled like twenty-four-karat gold. No doubt about it, this guy was a lady-killer.

He spoke in an intimate tone pitched for her ears alone. “Thank you for coming back to see me today and thank you for not betraying my identity. I owe you my life.”

His face was partially hidden in deep shadows. Beneath his swollen bruises and the big white bandage over his nose, she caught a glimpse of the man he normally was—a man so beautiful it almost hurt to look at him.

“Dang,” she murmured. “No wonder you’re on the list of the world’s most eligible bachelors.”

Oops. Had she just said that aloud? Oh, God. She had. She watched in dismay as he threw his head back and let out a rich laugh.

He gazed warmly at her. “Thank you for that. It was the best medicine you could have brought me today.”

Katy heard the lock rattle on the door. No doubt Riki had come to investigate why a prisoner was guffawing in here. She started as Nick’s hand shot out and he snatched at her veil. She’d forgotten about it being down. The heat from his touch on her cheek made her draw a sharp breath. His gaze jerked to hers, and he looked as startled as she felt. Quickly he tucked the veil back in place over her face.

He swore under his breath, then muttered, “Come visit me tomorrow if you can. I have something important to talk with you about.”

And then he drew away to the far end of the ledge and assumed a beaten-down posture just as the unpleasant guard from yesterday burst through the door.

"What's going on in here?" he demanded in French.

Katy stammered, "Uh, I had to check this prisoner's ribs for broken bones, and he's ticklish. It's all right."

The guard's suspicious gaze shifted back and forth between her and Nick.

Katy picked up her medical bag and stood. "I'm done in here for today," she told the guard. *What does Nick Ramsey want to talk with me about?* Surely he knew the limitations on any favors she could do for him as long as he was a prisoner of war. What else was there for them to discuss?

Curiosity always had been her downfall. She was the proverbial cat, and it killed her every time. And now she had to wait another whole day to find out what was on his mind. She felt like cursing under her breath, too.

It was a challenge, but she managed to walk out of the cell without looking back at the king in rags behind her.

The women huddled in a corner of the market. They dared not stand together for more than a few seconds lest they attract attention from the Army troops patrolling the city arrogantly.

"Did you contact a member of the InterAid team, Hanah?" one of them whispered.

"Yes. There's a girl on the team. Young. Pretty. She has kind eyes. Of all the aid workers, I think she'd be most likely to help us."

"Did she say she would work with us?"

"I haven't asked her directly yet."

"You must, Hanah. And hurry. Did you hear the Army arrested a woman for refusing to wear religious garments this morning? They say she's going to be punished as a whore."

The other women sucked in shocked breaths through their teeth.

A male voice rang out behind them. "You women there, be on your way! Meetings are forbidden!"

The women started as one and scattered quickly as the soldier slapped a riding crop against his leather boot.

The walk home from Il Leone was hot and dusty. Some sort of demonstration blocked the square Katy and Larry had passed through last night, and today the pair were forced to detour several blocks through winding, narrow cobblestone streets that were clearly relics from the twelfth century or so.

Thankfully her crusty coworker had a good sense of direction. Katy was completely turned around when they finally emerged on what appeared to be the other side of the jammed square. The crowd, whose backs were turned to them, struck her as odd. And then it dawned on her. It was completely silent. Intense. They acted as if they were watching something. Avidly.

"What's going on?" she murmured to Larry.

"Dunno. Stay here." She waited nearly a block away from the edge of the crowd while her ever-brash companion walked up to one of the men at the back of the crowd and put his hand on the guy's shoulder. The poor

Baraqi about fainted in his surprise. Folks were jumpy these days in Akuba.

And then she heard a woman scream. It rang of terror and pain and something else. Fury. What in the world was going on? Why had that woman screamed? And why was no one apparently doing anything to help her? There must be a thousand men crammed into that square.

The woman made another noise, this time more of a keening wail than a scream. The crowd surged forward, taking on a life of its own. The now-seething mass of humanity heaved forward, and Katy watched in horror as Larry was swallowed up by it and sucked forward. He disappeared from view, struggling backward to no avail against the crowd who pushed into the square.

Oh, God. Now what? She was standing out here all alone on a street corner, only vaguely aware of what direction to go to get back to her hotel. This couldn't be good. A new edict had come out that morning, something about women not going out unescorted into public places. Not good at all.

She jumped as a male voice practically snarled in her ear. "Get out of here. This is no sight for a lady."

She spun around, shoving her veil back into place as it half fell over her eyes. A soldier stood there scowling at her. Yet, as harsh as his words and demeanor were, she sensed a certain rough concern beneath them. *What* was no sight for a lady?

"Where is your chaperone?" the soldier demanded. "He should know better than to leave you alone like this. You could end up in the square next."

What was this guy talking about?

A veiled woman hurried up to the two of them. "Ah, Selima, there you are, sister. I thought I'd lost you in the crush. Come. Let us get back inside until the…spectacle…is over and the crowd disperses."

Katy nodded, afraid to speak in her foreign-accented Arabic and give herself away. So far, this soldier and the woman seemed to have mistaken her for a local. And her gut instinct was it would be unwise to disabuse them of the notion. For good measure, she stepped close to the other woman.

"Be gone with you," the soldier commanded them.

The woman grabbed her elbow and steered her down the street a little ways and into a small grocery store. They stopped just inside the doorway.

"What were you thinking, standing alone in public like that?" the woman hissed in French.

Katy stared. Why had this lady just transitioned into another language with her? "Uh, ma'am, I'm not your sister," she replied carefully.

"Of course you are not. You are the American relief worker."

Katy stared. "Who are you?"

The stranger pulled aside her veil, and Katy was suddenly looking at the receptionist from the hotel's front desk. "Hanah?"

The young woman nodded and hastily rearranged her veil, looking around furtively. "Come with me." She headed for the back of the store.

Katy followed, roundly confused. It was probably stupid to head off alone to who knows where like this, but it couldn't be any more dangerous than standing on that corner so close to an agitated mob. Plus, there was no sign whatsoever of Larry. He'd been completely swallowed by that writhing snake nest of humanity outside.

Hanah led Katy quickly out a back exit of the store and down a fetid alley. They turned a pair of corners, and then the Baraqi woman slipped into a doorway, this one leading into the back of an ancient stone building with high, small windows.

"In here," she urged.

Katy ducked under the low lintel and straightened as she looked around a primitive kitchen. A fireplace a person could stand in dominated one side of the room, along with a large brick oven the shape of a beehive and about as tall as she was. Then there was the incongruous sight of a refrigerator-freezer and a dishwasher on the other side of the room.

"We'll wait here. There is someone who needs to speak with you."

"About what?" Katy asked. There went her curiosity again.

"We shall wait."

And they did. Not for long, though. Maybe five minutes. And then another woman burst in through the same door they'd used. She took one look at Katy and huddled with Hanah for a whispered exchange.

Katy was alarmed when Hanah nodded, pulled on her veil and slipped outside, leaving Katy alone with this stranger. This woman took off her head scarf and veil and turned to face Katy.

She was elegantly attractive, probably a very well-maintained sixtysomething-year-old. Katy hadn't expected such a sophisticated-looking woman under the veil. But then, Baraq was a country full of surprises.

"Sit, please, Miss McMann. I'd like to speak with you."

The woman had spoken in English. American-accented, native-language, fluent English. What was an *American* doing living in a place like this?

Katy took off her head coverings and breathed a sigh of relief to be out from under the confines of the swathed layers of cloth. "Who are you?" she asked.

"My name is not important."

"Do you live here?" Katy blurted. It was probably rude to ask personal questions of a total stranger, but this woman was an anomaly in the current setting.

"Good heavens, no!" the woman exclaimed in genuine horror.

"Then what in the world are you doing here? It's not safe for an American like you to be here!" Katy responded.

"I have personal reasons for being here."

The woman's eyes had dimmed as she'd said these words, as if her personal problem were a grave one, indeed. Katy held her tongue and didn't pry.

The woman continued, "At the moment, my purpose is to speak to you on behalf of all Baraqi women—or at least most of them. Normally I wouldn't call myself an activist, but sometimes a person can't stand by and do nothing in the face of a great enough injustice."

A women's-rights activist from America. *Here?* This was one brave woman. At least Katy had the protection of InterAid while she was here.

Katy sat down at the massive scarred kitchen table and watched her impromptu hostess grab a towel and heft a cauldron of hot water from over the fireplace. She filled a pair of mugs and dipped tea bags into both.

The woman carried the cups to the table and stirred sugar into both at Katy's nod. "Don't drink the local water," the woman advised. "American digestive tracts can't take the bacteria. But this is safe."

Katy took a sip of the strong tea. It was bitter, but its tang and sweetness made for a tasty contradiction. Kind of like this country and the woman before her. A study in contrasts.

"Why do you wish to speak to me?" Katy asked.

"I wish for you to help the women of Baraq."

"How?"

The woman didn't answer directly. Rather, she took a long sip of her tea and then said, "Do you know what's happening in a public square a few blocks from here?"

The crowd of men and the screaming woman. "No."

"Several women are being publicly flogged."

Katy's eyes widened in horror. "Why?" she exclaimed.

"Because they refused to put on the *abaya* and *hijab.* They said General Sharaf has no right to force women behind the veil. Baraq is a modern nation ruled by secular law, and they cannot be forced to wear such garb against their will. And the general had them whipped for their protest."

The screams she'd heard came back to Katy and sent a shudder down her spine. It was barbaric. It was also not her job to get involved in such politics. She was here to monitor the treatment of prisoners for InterAid and nothing more.

But it was outrageous that any woman would be

flogged for something as simple as showing her face, when just days ago any woman in Baraq could've shown not only her face but her arms, hands, legs and feet in public if she liked!

The kernel of disquiet that had formed in Katy's gut over the ill treatment of the prisoners blossomed into full-blown anger. The regime of General Sharaf was not good for this country or its people.

But it wasn't as if there was anything she could do about it.

Other than hide the identity of the king and help him survive for as long as possible.

Oh, yeah. That.

As heavy as the burden of her secret might lie on her shoulders, she suddenly welcomed it. She would help Nikolas Ramsey no matter how dangerous doing so might be.

She leaned forward across the table. "How can I help?"

The woman smiled. "Hanah judged you correctly. She thought you might be willing to help us."

"I don't know what I can do, but I cannot sit by while women are punished for exercising their legal rights."

Fear glistened for a moment in the woman's eyes. She rose from the table and peered out the kitchen window and then into the hallway leading from the kitchen to the rest of the house. She returned and sat, leaning so close that Katy smelled the recent tea on the woman's breath. Apparently whatever she was about to say was exceedingly dangerous to utter aloud.

"You can help us find the king."

Katy's heart skipped a beat. "Find the—?"

The woman clapped a hand across Katy's mouth.

She nodded her understanding that she mustn't repeat the words aloud, and the woman lifted her hand away. Panic closed Katy's throat. Nick had been clear—no one must know he lived, and she must trust no one. Had she somehow given away his identity to someone watching her?

The woman at the table whispered urgently, "We have reason to believe he is not dead. He must be found."

"Why do you think he's alive?"

"Soldiers who were there when the throne room fell have said they saw a man who looked a great deal like him being carried out as a prisoner."

Crud. Did Nick know anyone had seen him? Were his hopes for staying hidden completely blown? "And what will you do if and when you find him?" Katy asked aloud.

"We will do our best to save him. Perhaps there is a way to get him away from Sharaf's men—if they have him—or to sneak him out of the city to safety, if he's in hiding. He may not be the best king, but he is a Ramsey. And he would never beat women in the streets."

Katy couldn't help herself. "How do you know he wouldn't be a decent king? He only sat on the throne for a week. It's awfully hard to judge someone in so short a time. Perhaps he wouldn't be half-bad if he were given a chance."

The woman gave Katy a long, hard look. For her part, Katy did her best to look innocent, as if her comment had been just a casual observation. She had to watch what she said to this lady. The woman was *very* sharp.

"You may be right, Miss McMann. You may be

wrong. But I do know he cannot be a worse ruler than Sharaf and his cronies."

Katy couldn't argue with that.

"If you find him, you must tell us," the woman insisted. "Then we can form a plan to protect him. Hopefully to get him out of the country."

Katy took a sip of her tea and studied her companion. An undertone of desperation vibrated in this woman's words. She smelled of fear. It oozed from her like a film of sweat. Katy felt a need to distract this woman from the sudden terror overwhelming her. "Where are you from?"

"Originally Connecticut. I picked up any British accent you hear at Oxford. That, and I have a home in London."

"What did you study?" Katy asked in surprise.

"Philosophy." The woman laughed lightly. "A fat lot of good that does me now."

No kidding. The woman was huddling in a dingy kitchen, heating water over a wood fire and whispering of conspiracy just so she could show her face in the street again. The desperation of the situation for all women in this country was personified in this educated, sophisticated woman living in Medieval squalor.

Did she dare break her promise to Nick and tell someone he was alive? Her intuition said this woman was trustworthy. But common sense said not to mention anything of his existence even to this woman, as passionate as she might be. Protecting Nick was not the other woman's fight to fight. At least not yet. Katy hoped the woman wouldn't notice that she was dodging answering. No such luck.

"Will you help us?" the woman demanded.

"I will do what I can to help you and the women of Baraq."

And to help Nick, she promised herself silently.

"Let us hope you can deliver the miracle we need to avert disaster."

Katy met the woman's gaze head-on. "For now, I think you and your friends need to put all your energy into devising a way to smuggle the king out of Baraq. From what I've seen of the Army so far, you may need a miracle or two of your own to accomplish that."

The woman raised her cup of tea to Katy in a grim toast. "Here's to miracles, then."

Nick measured time in the dungeon's perpetual gloom by the arrival of his twice-daily meals. A plate of watery gruel was passed in to him, announcing the arrival of morning. He washed down the tasteless mess with a dipper of water from the bucket that, since InterAid's arrival, had been reasonably clean.

With luck, Katy would come see him today. He rehearsed his speech to her several times, delivering it silently to the four walls surrounding him. He tried several approaches, but damned if he knew the best way to convince an American woman to go along with his insane plan. Women of that nationality were famously independent and strong-willed. He was just going to have to brazen it out and rely on her attraction to him to get her to say yes.

If only he'd made a habit of seducing young, softhearted Americans! But alas, he'd stuck to fast, hard women who knew the rules in his world: have fun, have sex, but never, ever fall in love.

In all his years of romancing women, he never could've imagined that one day *the future of his family name* would ride on his skills of seduction. But that day had come, and all of a sudden he felt completely unprepared to seduce the one woman he desperately needed to.

His entire life had turned into one giant irony. Somewhere the Fates were having a hell of a laugh at his expense. He only prayed they took pity on him and granted him this one small thing. *Please let Katy McMann say yes.*

He'd repeated that thought so many times through the night he'd lost count.

A tapped-out message from the cell next door announced the arrival of the American woman in the cell block sometime in the early afternoon. He passed on the message to the next cell and then sat down heavily on his stone ledge, so relieved that she'd come he could hardly stand.

It was time.

In a few minutes, Katy McMann would either save his soul or damn him to eternal hell.

He paced impatiently until the padlock finally rattled on his cell door. He leaped onto his ledge, assuming his usual submissive pose for the guard.

As he watched her walk into his cell from under his lowered eyelids, Nick experienced a moment of extraordinary clarity. It was going to be okay. Regardless of whether or not she accepted his offer, he would not go entirely alone into whatever destiny awaited him. This warm, kind, bright young woman would stand beside him. Of that he had no doubt. She would walk the last few weeks of his life with him.

It was a humbling gift. And it made him feel like an even bigger schmuck for what he was about to ask of her.

They exchanged murmured greetings and she made a report of his health while the surly guard lingered in the cell, eavesdropping. *Bastard.* It was almost as if the jerk sensed that he and Katy wanted to talk about something today, and the guy was determined not to let it happen! Nick curbed his impatience. It didn't do to make that particular guard mad. He had heavy fists and loved to use them. Nick had a couple new bruises on his ribs to show for it, in fact.

Katy detailed Prisoner 1806's progress with painstaking precision on her clipboard until finally, after an eternity, the guard left.

Nick sagged in relief.

With a furtive glance at the locked door, Katy pulled her veil away from her face and rolled her eyes. "I didn't think he was ever going to leave!"

Nick smiled. She really was very attractive. She still carried the softness of youth about her face, but she was the kind of woman who would be beautiful at thirty or sixty or ninety. He hadn't been kidding. She had great bones.

"How are you?" she asked, moving close to him.

"You already asked me that."

"Yes, but that was for the guard. How are you really doing?"

He frowned, considering the question. "Scared, mostly."

"I don't blame you. These Army guys are serious jerks. You won't believe what I passed yesterday on the way home—"

He cut her off gently. "I'm not afraid of *them.*"

"Then who?" Her eyes went big and round.

So damned innocent, she was. A spear of guilt pierced his gut. He closed his eyes on the pain for a moment. He had to do this. He *had* to.

"You."

"Me?"

He took a deep breath. "There's something I need to ask you."

She gazed at him curiously.

Duty, dammit! He owed this to his people. He stood and paced the cell restlessly, trying futilely to gather his thoughts. Uncharacteristically words completely failed him.

"Please, you can tell me anything," she murmured. "I'll keep your secrets."

Aah, sweet Katy. The vise around his chest loosened. "I have a favor to ask of you. A huge one. It is dangerous and foolish and I have no right to ask it of you. No right at all. But I must."

"What is it?"

His throat closed upon the words and he had to swallow before he could continue.

"Do you want me to help you escape?" she whispered, her eyes wide.

He smiled wryly. "If only it was something as insignificant as that."

"What in the world could be more significant than that?" She looked up at him in confusion.

He took a deep breath. "I want you to have my baby."

Chapter 5

Katy jerked sharply as if she'd been struck. She stared in utter amazement at the man standing before her. A myriad of images flashed through her head. Nick naked and inside her. Her abdomen swollen and heavy. A tiny, dark head suckling at her breast. Ohmigosh.

"Your *what!*" she exclaimed.

"You heard me correctly," he answered quietly.

"A *baby?*" The reason for such a request simply refused to compute in her brain. "Whatever for? Have you completely lost your mind?" she demanded.

She jumped up and paced the cell, too agitated to stand still. Good grief! She'd taken this job to help ease human suffering, not to be propositioned. By a deposed king. In jail!

She was startled when gentle hands grasped her shoulders, halting her circuits around the tiny space.

"Stop for a minute. Listen to me. Please."

She searched the depths of his eyes in the poor light. He didn't *look* crazy.

"It is only a matter of time until I'm recognized. When the rebels find out who I am, they'll kill me." His voice vibrated with urgency. "I'm the only remaining Ramsey. My father was an only child and I'm an only child. I have no direct living relatives. When I die, the Ramsey dynasty dies with me."

His gaze was compelling. Sincere.

Oh. My. God. *He isn't kidding.*

Her fingers went numb and her knees suddenly weren't all that steady.

He continued. "The people of Baraq have followed a Ramsey for a thousand years. We've been through conquerors, plague, famine and war together, and always the Baraqis and Ramseys have stood by one another."

He paced an agitated lap of his own around the cell. "This Army coalition is going to fall apart in a few months. I've met the generals involved. I saw them in action last week. They'll revolt against Sharaf's heavy hand. And before long, they'll start bickering among themselves and wrestling for personal power. In the process, they'll tear whatever government they've built apart."

Katy frowned. Don Ford had made a similar comment about the Army's commanders under his breath at breakfast.

Nick continued, "When that happens, the people of Baraq are going to need something—someone—to rally around. That person has always been a Ramsey. If there were an heir, a child for them to pin their hopes on, they'd have a reason to pick themselves up and go forward, to throw off the yoke of a man like Sharaf. I owe it to my people to leave them a promise for the future."

Katy simply stared. He wasn't asking her for his own life. Far from it. He'd made not one complaint about his imminent death in the impassioned speech he'd just given her. He was asking her this favor on behalf of his people. An entire nation of them. To give them a chance at something other than women being flogged in a square, at continuing a long and proud legacy of peace and prosperity. To give them a gift of hope.

The playboy had come a very long way in a very short time, apparently. His request was completely selfless. An act of generosity toward his people. It was the act of a king.

It was also completely out of the question.

She looked up to find his gaze burning at her like the sun's rays, so intense it was hard to look at.

"Nick, what you're asking is impossible."

"Why?" he demanded.

"Well, you're a king—"

"I'm a man," he interrupted.

"—and I'm a…a commoner." The word felt strange in her mouth.

"And you're a woman," he countered.

"I'm from the United States and you're from a totally different culture halfway around the world," she protested.

"It worked for Prince Rainier and Grace Kelly," he argued.

"They were both Christian, and she was a movie star. Used to glamour and glitz. I'm a plain old social worker."

"I'm about to be executed, and we're locked in a prison cell at the moment. Don't you think social status is rather meaningless in the circumstances?" he reasoned. "Besides, you are neither plain nor old."

"We don't even know if it—" her mind stumbled at the thought of making love with this man "—would work."

"That is true. I ask only for a chance to leave an heir. I would die in peace knowing I had tried."

"The whole idea is preposterous, Nick."

"Undoubtedly," he answered calmly.

"It's insane!"

"Agreed." He smiled warmly at her.

"I hardly know you."

"You are right. This is happening very fast. Too fast for civilized people like you and me. But I have no time, and you are the only woman I am likely to see before I die. It is my extreme good fortune that you are bright, kind and compassionate, not to mention single and attractive."

"I…I'm flattered…." she stumbled, at a loss for words. "I don't know what to say."

"Say yes. Think about it overnight if you have to. But I beg you, don't turn me down. Consider it the last request of a dying man. The last request of a dying nation."

She blinked, taken aback. When he put it like that, it was hard to imagine refusing him.

He stepped near and touched a strand of loose hair that had crept out of her ponytail. "Your hair is exactly the color I imagined it would be the first time I saw you," he murmured. "Gold, like a beach kissed by the setting sun."

Gently he tucked the strand of hair behind her ear, caressing the ticklish shell of her ear with a light touch. When he stood so close like this, she could hardly breathe.

"I ask only one thing of you, Katy. Do not think on your answer for too long. My time is very short. A few days maybe. A few weeks if I'm lucky."

She nodded and drew breath to speak, when abruptly the padlock outside the door rattled. The guard had returned.

She took a quick step back and replaced her facial veil. Her last sight of Nick as the cell door swung closed was him standing tall and straight in the center of the room. He inclined his head toward her, a regal movement of homage.

A baby. *A baby! Nick's* baby. She loved kids. But what of this child? What destiny awaited Nick's heir? Did she have what it took to nurture and educate such a child? To raise a prince or princess to lead a nation out of chaos? She'd be a single parent. Her folks would be mortified, but they'd help her anyway. They were already bugging her about when she was going to settle down and give them grandchildren. Although this was undoubtedly *not* what they had in mind.

Good Lord. She was actually considering the idea.

He was right that the people of Baraq needed a Ramsey heir. Women's rights were being trampled left and right under Sharaf. She had no doubt that if the Baraqis had an alternative to the repressive Army regime, they'd leap at it.

The cries of those women in the square haunted her,

along with the feverish fear of the woman sitting in that kitchen, begging for Katy's help. She couldn't turn her back on the women of this nation.

But she barely knew Nick! And to have his baby?

Although, what she knew of him wasn't all bad. He was facing his imminent death with an equanimity she couldn't have mustered in the same circumstances. He was more concerned about his people's future than his own. And it didn't hurt that he was gorgeous and charming, either.

It was preposterous even to consider his proposition. But considering it she was.

Katy fumbled through the rest of her day, nodding absently and pretending to listen to the complaints and woes of the other prisoners.

Larry Grayson gave her a funny look when she skipped supper and went straight up to her room that night. But thankfully he didn't try to stop her and ferret out what was on her mind.

Katy stripped out of her *abaya* and veils the second her door closed, grateful for the feel of air directly upon her skin. The black robes became suffocating after a while. She couldn't imagine a lifetime trapped under them.

She took a tepid sponge bath in her room in lieu of waiting for the floor's lone bathtub to become available, and she crawled into bed early.

She stared at the ceiling for what had to be most of the night. Nick needed an answer right away. But no matter how hard she tried, she couldn't arrive at a decision. There was no doubt his proposition was for a noble and worthy cause. But the idea of her having the baby of a doomed Arab prince was just too strange to wrap her mind around.

Nick Ramsey's baby. The child would undoubtedly be beautiful like its father. Intelligent. Athletic. Kind at heart. If she went to a sperm bank to pick a father for her child, she couldn't possibly come up with a better candidate than Nick Ramsey.

Except she wasn't in the market for a child.

Was she?

Her arms abruptly ached for the feel of a small, warm body nestled trustingly against her breast.

She tossed and turned, caught on the horns of her dilemma. One minute she'd argue herself out of doing it, and the next she'd argue herself right back into the idea.

For goodness' sake, she hadn't had a steady boyfriend since her sophomore year of college. She'd have to make love with Nick—and she'd only met the guy a couple days ago! The idea of getting naked in front of a man like him made her skin crawl with embarrassment. He'd think she was lumpy and ugly after all the supermodels he must have bedded.

But then her thoughts swung back the other way. Her upbringing might have been conservative, but she wasn't a complete prude. And it would be for a really good cause. If the women of Baraq could endure public floggings in order to protest their treatment at the hands of General Sharaf, she could endure making love with Nick Ramsey. She'd dreamed about that very thing only the previous night, after all. What was so bad about making the fantasy a reality? It had been a pretty good fantasy.

When pale light started to seep in her window the next morning, she gave up trying to sleep and got out of bed. She opened the window to catch whatever breeze moved outside.

A few trucks, mostly carrying fresh produce, began to rumble along the cobblestone streets below. Just as the first narrow slash of sun broke over the horizon, the nasal song of an imam calling the faithful to morning worship floated across the city. The sound was beautiful and mysterious, steeped in an ancient and rich tradition. Again she thought of how Akuba was an intriguing mix of new and old, east and west. So was its king.

She let the curtain drop and turned to get dressed. No matter how hard she willed it not to, the moment of reckoning was fast approaching.

Nineteen. Twenty. Nick touched his chin briefly to the bars covering his tiny window in one last pull-up before he dropped to the floor. His arms ached, but he stretched out on his ledge anyway and did push-ups until he could not lift himself another time.

He collapsed, sweating, against the cold rock. Some romantic bed it was going to make if Katy agreed to his proposition. He briefly pictured his sumptuous chambers several floors above in the palace and then pushed the image out of his mind. He would not experience such luxury again before he died. It did no good to dwell on what he'd lost and depress himself.

Katy had to agree to have his baby. She *had* to.

Not only did he have to get across that hurdle with

her somehow, but he also had to get her to agree to marry him. If the child was to be his legitimate heir, it had to be conceived in wedlock.

He hadn't broached that part of the plan with her yesterday. One shock at a time. Fortunately she'd reacted much less violently than she might have. At least she hadn't turned him down outright. He held out hope that her innately kind nature and desire to help those in need would trump her common sense. For surely she'd be insane to accept his proposition.

Slowly his pulse returned to normal after his vigorous workout. He took a long drink of water from his bucket and then used the last bit of it to sponge himself off. God, he'd pay a fortune for a hot shower.

Stop it, he ordered himself. No regrets. No longings for things he couldn't have. Live in the moment. *Live for the Baraqi people.*

He jumped as the padlock abruptly rattled. He whirled in anticipation but was disappointed when a robed male figure stepped into the room.

"Mr. Mulwami?" the man asked.

Nick started. He knew that voice. Kareem Hadar! He bowed slightly to the religiously garbed man. "Praise Allah, I am Akbar Mulwami," he said for the benefit of the guard, who was just backing out of the cell.

"It is my duty to visit the prisoners and see to the welfare of their immortal souls." Kareem stepped away from the door as it closed. "It is good to see you alive and well, Your Highness.

"Don't call me that," Nick snapped with a quick glance at the door.

"Sorry. Old habits are hard to break." Kareem bowed his head in apology. "How do you fare?"

"Better than might be expected. Tell me—how much access to the palace do you have?"

"The Army believes I support their cause. And they haven't found the secret passages yet. With a bit of care, I can go just about anywhere in the palace. Why? What do you need?"

"Is there any chance at all that we could mount an escape from Il Leone and live?"

"None. Our people have been working on it ever since you were captured, and Sharaf has this place locked up tighter than a drum. I am sorry. My plan to keep you alive has merely delayed your death, I am afraid."

"I'm the one who chose to stay on and take the throne after my father died. Do not blame yourself."

The two men were silent for a moment.

Then Nick murmured, "Can you gain access to the air shaft that leads to this cell?"

The older man frowned. "I suppose so. It must run past the south receiving hall, which is directly above this. I could get in there and get near the window. Why?"

"I need you to hear something through the shaft."

Kareem looked confused. "Pray tell, what is it you need me to hear?"

"My wedding vows."

The older man jolted. "Your *what?* Do you expect to marry thin air? Or mayhap a ghost who haunts your cell?"

Nick grinned. "Not at all. I expect to marry a very much alive and breathing young woman. An American who works for InterAid. Either tomorrow afternoon or the day after. As I recall, all that is required under ancient Islamic tradition for a wedding to be valid is for the bride and groom to repeat their vows to each other three times in front of witnesses."

Kareem stared at him as if he'd gone completely mad. Maybe he had. "That is an old custom, but you are essentially correct. Won't the American woman be Christian, though?"

Nick nodded. "Probably. She can repeat the Christian marriage vows to me if she likes, and I'll do the Muslim ones to her."

"It's shaky legally."

"Actually, it's mostly shaky religiously. Baraqi law says the king may recognize any voluntary union between two people as a legal and binding marriage. As far as I know, I'm still technically king of Baraq. No act of parliament has attempted to dethrone me, has it?"

"No," Kareem answered bitterly. "Sharaf has taken no action to make this coup of his legal. If he tried, he'd have a hell of a time succeeding. I've got most of the avenues he could try completely blocked." Kareem hesitated for a moment, then asked, "How did you get the American girl to agree to this plan, anyway?"

Nick shrugged. "It's a long story. Too long for the time we have. And she hasn't exactly agreed to it yet. I can only hope she'll marry me and make an attempt to have an heir before I die. But just in case, I need you to be ready to witness the vows and record them properly. This wedding must be completely legal and binding. If any heirs issue from this union, there must be no question of our marriage's validity down the road. Do you understand?"

The older man nodded solemnly, respect blossoming beside the incredulity in his gaze. "I do. A creative plan, under the circumstances."

Nick shrugged. "A crazy plan. But it's the best I can do for my people under the circumstances."

Kareem smiled warmly. "It is good to hear you speak that way. I will do whatever I can to assist you."

Nick stepped forward to place an affectionate hand on Kareem's shoulder. "I cannot tell you how much this means to me, my friend."

The two men exchanged candid looks. They both knew Nick was going to die. Soon. But it felt good to have a plan. To have something to *do*. Even if it was an absurd plan, it was better than just sitting back and waiting for the inevitable.

Nick spoke again quickly. Time was against him, and this might be his only chance to talk to Kareem before…well, before. "When I am gone, I want you to open my private safe and take everything inside it for yourself. I bequeath it all to you. Consider it payment for this last service to me and my family. You have been a true and loyal supporter of the House of Ramsey. This is the combination to the lock…."

Nick rattled off a series of numbers and had Kareem repeat them back to him several times.

Before Nick could give the older man any further instructions, the guard returned to announce that their time was up. As the older man was escorted out, Nick threw a significant look over his shoulder at the tiny air vent, and Kareem nodded back almost imperceptibly.

The day dragged by slowly, and afternoon came

and went with no sign of Katy. Nick was alarmed. Had she decided not to come back? Was this her answer to his question?

He'd well and truly failed his country, then. Despair settled upon him, a dark, suffocating cloak that snuffed out his last spark of hope. The starkness of his prison cell matched his mood as the sun set and his cell grew dark.

And then, without warning, the padlock rattled.

A rush of air filled his lungs. Could it be?

A whisper of silk announced Katy's arrival as she swept through the door. She stopped to pass a small bag to the guard, a boy of no more than fourteen or so by the looks of him. And then they were alone.

Nick held his breath, not daring to hope.

"I'm sorry I'm so late," she said in a rush as she stepped into the cell. "I waited until that nasty guard who was on duty this morning left. Riki—he's the boy who let me in here—is much nicer." Her voice dropped low. "He agreed to let me have a few extra minutes with you and not tell anyone."

Nick frowned. "What does he want in return?"

"Honey cakes."

"Honey cakes?" Nick echoed, surprised.

"The hotel our team is staying at makes them. They're too sweet for me, so I put mine in my bag every morning and bring them for Riki. He's so young. A child, really. He adores them."

Nick shook his head. Thank God for small favors and the ingenuity of the young woman standing before him.

To his surprise, she pulled off her entire veil and

shook her head. A cascade of glorious spun gold swirled around her face.

"I have to admit that I'm tired of the whole veil thing. It's tolerable for about one day and then it gets old. Really old. I can't imagine how the women of Baraq are going to stand it for the long-term."

Nick frowned. "Under the rule of my family, women weren't required to wear such garments. The women of Baraq must be furious that the Army drove them back behind the veil."

Katy winced. "Actually, the local women I've talked to are more frightened than angry. They're terrified of what other rights the Army regime will take away from them. Sharaf actually had a bunch of women flogged when they refused to wear *abayas* and veils."

Nick slapped his palm against the wall with a loud crack. "Damn! If only I'd had more time."

Katy put a sympathetic hand on his arm. "I'm so sorry this is happening to you and your country."

He smiled ruefully. "It's not your fault. It's mine."

"Don't be so hard on yourself, Nick."

He snorted and spun away from her comforting touch. "That's easy for you to say."

She sat down on the edge of the stone ledge. "Did you get any sleep last night?" she asked.

"Not a wink," he admitted.

"You need to take care of yourself," she said, empathetic as always.

"I've got all eternity to sleep," he replied dryly. "How about you? Did you get any rest?"

"Not really," she confessed.

He sighed. "I apologize for throwing you into such a quandary with my request. It's not fair of me and you didn't ask for it."

"You didn't ask for a coup d'état, either," she replied.

He moved the few steps to her side and sat on the ledge. He pushed the knuckle-length sleeves of her *abaya* out of the way and grasped her hands. As he'd expected, they were ice-cold. He noticed they were also elegantly shaped and satin-soft.

"In a way, I did ask for it. If I had come home more often, taken an interest in Baraq sooner… I've made so many mistakes…." He swore under his breath.

She murmured, "You can't let regret overwhelm you. We can only learn from our mistakes and move forward."

She squeezed his fingers, and her palms molded to his the same way lovers' bodies might mold to one another. A need to feel her, flesh to flesh, head to toe, nearly overcame him. A faint tremor passed through her fingers.

"You're not afraid of me, are you?" he asked, dismayed.

"No," she replied candidly. "I'm afraid of myself."

"Why?" He released one of her hands and traced the beautiful shape of her cheek. "There's nothing for you to fear from me."

Her breath caught and she bit her lip. He stared at the moistness of her lower lip. "Aah, Katy," he breathed. "I am a moth to your flame. You bring light into my darkness."

She let out a sigh.

That gentle breath of air fanned a veritable inferno inside him. He'd love nothing more than to sweep her up in his arms and plunder her mouth, to have her unfold beneath him, giving everything he asked and more, her generosity in love as large as her heart in life. He had no right to take any of this from her, but how could he not? She was life itself and he was a dying man.

The dark walls of his prison faded away, replaced by the wide-open spaces of the desert. Her hair was the golden sand, her eyes the deep blue sky, her laughter the wind that cooled his heated flesh, her gentle spirit the water that slaked his thirst.

When had he suddenly waxed so poetic? Or was it just hallucinations from lack of sleep and proper nutrition? Or maybe this was what happened to the mind when it faced impending death.

As much as he wanted to savor this moment, to draw out the pleasure of looking at her and touching her for as long as he could, time was his enemy. The guard would be back soon. He had to break the spell.

"Katy, I would like to stand here and gaze into your eyes for an eternity. But I am afraid that time marches on. Young Riki will be back any minute, if I don't miss my guess."

Regret shadowed her azure gaze.

He dropped his eyes in apology before he asked quietly, "Have you thought about my request?"

She laughed ruefully. "I haven't thought about anything else."

"And have you arrived at a decision?" He looked up at her intently. He had no wish to push her, but the suspense was most certainly going to kill him soon.

She gazed searchingly at him for a long moment. And then she sighed.

"Yes, Nick, I've made my decision."

Chapter 6

The prison's darkness swirled around Katy in a stormy vortex, Nick's golden gaze burning bright in the center of it. The moment imprinted itself on her memory forever. She faced a choice, a fork in the path that would significantly change her life no matter which direction she chose. This was all moving much too fast for her. But the one thing they didn't have was time.

"Well?" he prompted.

She took a deep breath. "I'll do it. I'll have your baby."

Nick's heartfelt sigh of relief was calming but also frightening. She had just set herself upon the more dangerous path of the two. Much more dangerous.

He stepped forward. "Thank you, Katy," he breathed as his arms went around her. He hugged her painfully tight, but she didn't mind. Her head rested comfortably upon his shoulder, and her arms crept around his waist. His body was big and hard against hers. Muscular. Masculine. And she'd just agreed to sleep with him. Trepidation flared in her gut.

She leaned back in his embrace and looked up at him. "Now what do we do?" she asked in a small voice.

He grinned down at her. "I thought they explained the birds and the bees early on to you American women."

Surprised out of her case of nerves, she laughed. "I've got that part down. I was wondering how and when we do this."

The smile faded from Nick's eyes. "There is one thing we must do first."

"What?"

"We must be married. For this child to be my legal heir, it must be conceived in wedlock."

Shock slammed into her. Married? Her? To *him?* "You want me to m-marry you?" she stuttered.

He frowned. "Is that such an onerous thought? I promise you'll be a safely available widow in no more than a few weeks."

The thought wrenched her heart. "I'm sorry. I didn't mean it like that," she corrected hastily. "It's just the idea of me marrying a guy like you… A king… It's kind of hard to imagine."

"Welcome to Cinderella's world," he said lightly.

Only one response to that came to mind. "Wow." And then she said, "How are we ever going to throw a wedding in here without getting caught? I don't see how we're going to manage that."

Nick replied, "Actually, I've taken care of it."

Already? Had he been that sure she'd accept his proposal?

"*Just in case,* I arranged for a witness to be at the other end of that air shaft tomorrow afternoon. The Muslim tradition is that if a man and woman state that they marry one another three times before a proper witness, the marriage is legal."

Katy glanced at the tiny opening. "Are you Muslim? I'm Christian. Won't that be a problem?"

He sighed. "I was born Muslim and raised Anglican, so take your pick. The thing is, we don't stand a chance of getting a minister in here to officiate a Christian wedding. But I can arrange a Muslim witness. Since the government of Baraq recognizes both Christian and Muslim religious ceremonies, I figured we could merge the two. We'll repeat Christian vows in the Muslim way."

"Will that be legal?" she asked doubtfully.

"All it takes for the wedding to be legal in Baraq is a civil marriage license signed by a government official of sufficient rank." Dryly he added, "Last time I checked, I have sufficient rank in the legitimate Baraqi government to qualify."

That made her laugh. And goodness knew, she needed the tension relief. This was all happening so blasted fast!

"If we say our vows into the air shaft, the gentleman above will hear them and witness them properly. The civil marriage license will have to catch up with you later, I'm afraid. I'll sign it as soon as it can be smuggled in to me, and then I can pass it to you or it can be sent to you later."

Later, as in after he was dead. Oh, God.

"I'm sorry, Katy. It was the best I could do."

She took a deep breath for courage, set aside her misgivings and said gamely, "I think it's amazing that you've managed to arrange all this."

He smiled painfully at her. It was the first glimpse of regret she'd seen from him. She stepped close and hugged him. "It'll be all right, Nick. This will work out. For both of us."

He sighed and then his spine straightened resolutely. "The important thing is that we know in our hearts that we are husband and wife. A marriage ultimately stands between us and God, anyway. Even if my friend doesn't succeed in getting you a copy of the marriage license, you'll still have DNA to prove the parentage of our child."

Katy frowned. "But if you have no living relatives, whose DNA will they compare the child's to?"

"Mine. It is likely my body will be buried and not burned. It is considered a great insult to bury a Muslim's body along with that of a pig. While I haven't practiced the faith for a long time, it is how I was raised as a child. I expect the rebels will want to insult me in such a fashion. You will have to insist that my remains be exhumed and DNA samples taken from it."

The thought of Nick dead made her positively ill. "Oh, Nick, isn't there something we can do to save you?" she cried softly.

He looked her straight in the eye. "No, Katy, there is not. That is why we must make a child together if we can."

She closed her eyes, steeling herself to continue with this agonizing conversation. "Okay, so I insist on DNA tests to prove that the child is yours. Then what?"

"Contact your government's State Department. Ask for the names of high-ranking members of my government who survived the coup and made it out of Baraq. Let them know my child lives. They will do the rest. I will give you a list of names of people who are staunch allies of the Ramsey throne."

Alarm cut through her. "They won't try to take the baby from me, will they?"

Nick jerked back and stared down at her. "Certainly not! You will be honored as my queen and you will raise our child."

Relief made her light-headed for a moment.

Nick continued. "Speaking of which, I want you to raise our baby in the United States. Teach this child about the West so he or she can bring Baraq into the modern world. It is my country's only hope of survival in the long run."

Katy gulped. Teach their baby all by herself to be a king or queen? It was a daunting thought.

Nick must have sensed her alarm. "You will not be alone. Friends of my family's, former advisors, wealthy Baraqis, they'll all be beating down your door to help you train and educate this child. If I had to guess, your worst problem will be too much help, not too little."

Katy smiled wryly. "You forgot to add my family to that list of well-meaning meddlers. My parents are beside themselves to become grandparents."

Nick gathered her close. "I'm sorry I won't be there to help you with this. I can only thank God a woman like you was delivered to me who is capable of taking on this challenge."

"You barely know me. How do you know I can do this?"

"You're here in Baraq, aren't you? How many women have the courage and compassion to travel halfway around the world to help total strangers in their time of need?"

Katy took a deep breath. Could she ever hope to live up to his expectations of her? "I'll do my best, Nick. I only hope it's enough."

"I have money in London. You'll need to contact my bank once you get out of Baraq and get the Ramsey holdings transferred to you. I'll give you the account numbers, passwords and a letter of reference. Those should be sufficient to get the funds released. There should be enough money to keep the two of you safe and well cared for until the child is grown. Besides," he added with a trace of bitterness, "I'll be damned if Sharaf is going to get his hands on my family's money."

Katy nodded, dazed at the enormity of what she was taking on.

"If you will bring a pen and paper for me tomorrow, I can write down the name and phone number of the bank and of a few Baraqis living abroad who you can count on to be loyal to you and the child."

"I have writing stuff in my bag now." Katy pulled out a small personal journal and a ballpoint pen and handed them to Nick.

He turned to a blank page and rapidly filled two full pages with names, addresses, phone numbers and banking information.

He handed the book back to her. "That should be enough to get you started. May I keep the pen and some paper overnight? There are a couple other documents I need to write before I die."

Katy gulped. Like a will. She tore a fistful of pages out of the book and handed them to him. She tucked the rest of the journal carefully into her medical bag.

"So when was the start of your last period?" Nick asked abruptly.

Katy started and looked up at him. Heat flooded her cheeks. She knew why he was asking, but the idea of discussing something so personal with anybody, let alone a man, and let alone *this* man, was embarrassing in the extreme. "Uh, about ten days ago," she managed to stammer.

"Excellent. But that means we have no time to waste."

The irony of his remark made Katy wince. He had no time at all. And she—she had a lifetime. Good Lord willing, two lifetimes. Hers and a child's. The good news was McMann women tended to get pregnant if their husbands even sneezed in the same county. She and Nick had a real shot at making a baby if her genes held true.

The padlock rattled outside. Nick stepped back hastily, while she grabbed her veil and wrapped it around her head.

"Come back tomorrow afternoon," he murmured as she swept past him to stand at the door of the cell.

"Count on it," she replied before she stepped out.

Nick prayed that Kareem had done as he'd promised and found the other end of the air shaft. He'd told the older man it would be afternoon when Katy came. Nick also prayed nothing would interfere with that, today of all days.

So many details, all of which had to fall into place perfectly for this scheme to work. It was a fragile house of cards at best. But it was his only chance. He just had to hope that somehow it all worked out. He offered up a rare prayer—to a Christian or Muslim god, he didn't care. Just so long as some divine entity heard him and took mercy on him. *Please, God, help me in this one last endeavor before I die.*

Nick counted the hours after breakfast anxiously. The light grew as bright as it ever did in his cell, indicating that midday had come.

Another bit of good luck: the surly guard whom Katy didn't like had gone off duty with the coming of afternoon. Hopefully bribable Riki of honey-cake fame was on shift today.

Please, God, let the timing of this work out.

Some wedding day this was turning out to be. And to think, he'd always wished to avoid a big, elaborate state wedding broadcast by satellite to half the world. He'd certainly gotten that wish. He alternately paced and lay down on his stone bed, his nerves stretched to nearly the breaking point. He'd done his best to wash himself and straighten his filthy clothes, but he wasn't presentable to swine, let alone to his bride. He sighed and got up to pace some more.

Finally, when the light had begun to wane from his window, the padlock outside rattled to announce someone's arrival. It was too early for supper. *Please, God, let it be Katy.*

Sure enough, her black robe swept into the room in a rush of lavender. He glimpsed a wrapped package changing hands between Katy and Riki before the cell door swung shut.

Nick folded her, robes and all, into a relieved embrace. "Thank goodness you're here. I was losing my mind waiting for you."

She hugged him back tightly. "Me, too. I didn't think I was ever going to get done with my other visits."

"I don't like sharing you with the other prisoners," Nick growled in abrupt jealously. "Good thing they're my subjects and I have to share or I'd tell you to stop seeing any of them."

Katy's bright blue gaze shined up at him, laughing. "A greedy king, are we?"

Nick grinned back. "Speaking of greed, what was in the package you gave to Riki?"

"Cosmetics for his mother and a whole bag of honey cakes for him."

Nick asked, surprised, "Cosmetics? We still have such things readily available here in Baraq."

The smile faded from Katy's gaze. "Not many. The new regime outlawed them."

The urgency of what they were about to do struck Nick afresh. He had to give his people an alternative to a repressive military dictatorship. The Baraqis would never stand for this sort of backward thinking if there were another ruler to be had.

Please, God, give us a child to lead my people out of darkness.

He held out his hand to her. "Come, Katy. It is time."

She laid her hand in his, and he led her the few steps to the far side of the cell, underneath the tiny window.

Katy looked up at him, her gaze apprehensive and trusting at the same time.

"How about if you give me your vows according to the Christian tradition, and I give you mine according to the traditions of Islam? That way both religions will be satisfied."

She smiled, relieved. "That sounds splendid. I'm not sure I can remember the whole wedding ceremony, but I can hit the high points."

"As long as you remember the 'I take you, Nick, to be my lawfully wedded husband' part, I think we'll be okay. You'll have to repeat that bit three times, though. That's the ancient Islamic way."

Katy nodded. "Three times. Got it. Does your ceremony have a similar line in it?"

"It does." In a mellow baritone Nick recited a line of beautiful Arabic that flowed over her like water.

"That was lovely," Katy sighed.

Nick smiled. "If we had more time, I'd read you poetry in Arabic. It is the most beautiful in all the world."

But he didn't have the time.

Awareness of that fact settled between them, and some of the light seemed to leave the room.

Nick turned to face her. She was lovely in the half-light. She looked as though she'd lost some weight in the past days. Her cheekbones were more pronounced, and the new thinness about her face made her eyes look even bigger and more blue. He took both of her ice-cold hands in his and gave them a gentle squeeze.

"If you're ready," he said quietly, "let's begin. Why don't you go first?"

Please, God, let Kareem hear this.

Katy nodded seriously. He gazed deeply into her eyes. No matter that this wasn't a huge cathedral. No matter that she wore a simple black *abaya* and not an elaborate white lace wedding gown. No matter that they were all alone. When she started into the familiar words, Nick's heart tripped and sped up.

"I, Katy, do take thee, Nikolas, to be my lawfully wedded husband..."

Her eyes shone as if a starry night had been captured within their blue depths. He gazed into them, losing himself completely as her words rolled over him, soothing him all the way to his soul. As bizarre as the circumstances were that had brought them to this moment, a feeling of rightness suffused him. This was the woman who'd been made for him, whom he'd been meant by destiny to marry. Even if they only had a short time together on this Earth, he was going to savor it and give her as much of himself and his heart as he could in whatever time they had.

"...to have and to hold in sickness and health..."

Her voice faltered. He squeezed her hands and gave her a reassuring smile. She took a deep breath and continued. What a brave young woman she was. Pride in her filled him.

"...until death..." Her voice cracked and then broke altogether. She swallowed and managed to choke out, "...until death do us part."

He smiled soothingly at her. She'd made it through, all the way to the end, complete with the three repetitions of the key lines.

"I'm sorry, Nick," she whispered.

"It's all right," he murmured. "In my vows, I will promise to be with you for eternity. Even death will not extinguish what we have between us."

She took a quick swipe at her nose and then smiled up at him through the tears swimming in her eyes.

He took a deep breath and began to recite his own marriage vows. They came haltingly at first, but as he continued in his mother tongue, the familiar Arabic phrases came more and more easily. Katy seemed mesmerized by his voice, and he spoke to her from the bottom of his heart. By the time he finished, he was all but delivering the words as a love song to Katy, his wife, his soul mate, his beloved for all time.

And then it was done. Silence fell between them and, wide-eyed, they looked at each other while the magnitude of the moment trembled between them like a perfect dewdrop on a newly bursting rose.

A slow smile broke across Katy's face. "In my religion," she murmured, "it is traditional for the groom to kiss the bride."

Nick felt an answering smile spread across his face. "It is the same in my religion."

He lowered his head and touched her warm, soft lips with his. She sighed and her arms went around his neck. He lost himself in the kiss, relishing the warm, sweet taste of her upon his tongue, the way her body went liquid against his, the way she gave and took at the same time, making him feel wanted and appreciated. He drew her close, offering his protection and his strength to lean on, offering the best that was within him. As he welcomed her into his heart, it seemed as if she did the same in return for him.

He tugged the veil completely off her head, freeing her golden hair to spill across his hands. She was his angel of light, bringing warmth and brightness into his world. He couldn't get enough of her.

He took a firm hold on his emotions and slowed himself down. He wasn't going to rush her. He lifted his head and took her by the hand. Slowly he led her to the ledge, where his lone blanket was neatly spread.

He reached for her throat and the fastenings that held her *abaya* closed. She watched him, rapt, as he undid them and then lifted the black fabric away from her.

He opened the robe's folds wide, like velvet wings unfurling, to reveal Katy, swathed in a plain white dress made of silk that clung to every curve and nuance of her body. The garment was completely unadorned, and her fair skin glowed like a diamond against the simple background of white silk.

She was curvaceous, and he reveled in the fact that she wasn't bony. Frankly he'd never found the thin angularity of high-fashion models all that appealing and he relished her womanliness. Katy was full of curves and hollows and shadowed places that begged to be explored.

"Beautiful," he breathed. Katy's rib cage relaxed as if she'd been holding her breath. He glanced up, surprised by the apprehensive look on her face. "What are you worried about?"

"That you'll think I'm fat and won't find me the least bit attractive. You're probably used to gorgeous, perfect women, but I'm just sort of average."

He smiled, amused. "Katy, my dear, you are anything but average. Actually, I was just thinking how relieved I am that you're not skin and bones. That's completely unattractive to me."

A smile relaxed her features. "Even if you don't mean that, it was nice of you to say it."

He chuckled and held out his arms to her. "Come. Let me show you whether or not I meant it."

She stepped forward shyly, and as she did, he stripped the *abaya* off her arms. He flung it wide, using it to cover the crude ledge, transforming it into an elegant and mysterious perch worthy of his wife.

His wife! Shockingly the words delighted him. He bent and picked her up in his arms, grinning at her gasp of surprise. He laid her on their marriage bed and followed her down, stretching out beside her, kissing her throat and inhaling the dusty-sweet scent of lavender as he did.

"I love the way you smell," he murmured.

Katy laughed softly. "Remind me to thank my soap company for their products."

He rose up on one elbow, relishing the humor she brought into his life. "I will."

She reached up for the buttons on his shirt. "I'm feeling a little underdressed here, Nick. Perhaps you wouldn't mind taking off some of your clothes?" she asked seriously.

"Where have my manners gone? Of course I'd be happy to strip for you, madam," he teased.

A shadow of apprehension touched her gaze, and he reminded himself sharply to go slowly with his bride. A frisson of guilt whisked through him for taking advantage of her like this—and for enjoying it so much. He vowed to make it up to her as best he could. If he had to seduce her, the least he could do was make it as pleasurable as possible. He'd never thought of making love as a selfless act before. But as soon as the concept occurred to him, he was struck by the power of the discovery.

And then her hands were on his skin, and he forgot all about anything but the wonder of her. She slid her palms across his chest, measuring the width of his shoulders, her murmur of approval stealing his breath clean away.

Tentatively she leaned forward to kiss his throat, and he delighted in the butterfly softness of her mouth. He shrugged out of his shirt and kicked off the rest of his clothes in a rush. He rolled over and literally stopped breathing when Katy's silk-clad body pressed against his. The sensation was exquisite. He closed his eyes, enthralled. She made a tiny movement that brought their bodies into even more perfect alignment with each other, and he thought he might burst on the spot.

His body screamed to be joined with hers, to be buried deep inside her softness and warmth. It was all he could do not to rip the silk fabric off her and take her that instant. She was his wife. He owed her his sanity, his life, his future legacy, everything. He most certainly owed her a full measure of pleasure, today of all days. Clamping down hard on his raging desire, he let his hands roam freely over her body. The silk glided beneath his fingers in a seductive slide that nearly sent him over the edge.

He leaned down, replacing his fingers with his mouth. He explored the valley between her breasts, bewitched by the way she arched into him, offering herself for more of the same. Through the wet silk, he felt her breasts tighten and contract, the hard nubs of her nipples proclaiming her pleasure. She moaned softly. He moved lower, savoring the ticklishness of her ribs, the flatness of her belly, the curve of her hip.

Where she ever got the notion she was average or even fat, he had no idea, because she was flawlessly shaped and proportioned for his taste. The Greek sculptors couldn't have done it any better.

Impatient to taste her flesh, he reached for the hem of her dress and raised it slowly, revealing her shapely legs inch by elegant inch. His mouth followed in the wake of the silk's retreat, tasting and learning her as he went. He searched out every secret of her body, seeking each place that gave her pleasure, each touch that made her gasp in delight, until he could restrain himself no longer.

Finally he raised himself over her, positioning himself between her soft thighs. He stroked the swollen slickness of her flesh until she sprawled in wanton pleasure and finally opened her eyes to plead.

"Please, Nick."

He did not need another invitation. He sank down into her brilliance, buried himself in her heat and light, the power of the moment sweeping him completely out of himself. Possessiveness roared through him. Forever he would be her husband and she his wife. When she joined him in paradise someday, they would be as one. They would hold each other's bodies and hearts for eternity.

He kissed her and caressed her until her body unclenched itself around him. Then ever so slowly he began to move inside her. As eager and generous as always, she wrapped her legs around him, pulling him closer, flying high with him. Their bodies and souls merged, breaking free of the stone walls around them, soaring straight up toward the sun, until the glory and power of it all but burned them to ashes.

He kissed her then, shouting the joy of his release into her mouth. He shuddered with the violence of it, humbled by the gift she'd given him.

Panting, he opened his eyes to gaze down at Katy. The wonder on her face was surely the most beautiful sight he'd ever seen. A single thought pierced his dazed and awed mind.

Thank you, merciful God, for answering my prayers.

Chapter 7

Katy finally remembered to breathe as she looked up at Nick. *Her husband.* The words felt foreign on her tongue but were sweet ambrosia nonetheless. Her relief was profound that he found her attractive and hadn't had to force himself to make love to her.

If she called anyone she knew back in the States and told them she'd just secretly married a handsome prince who was trapped in a castle dungeon by an evil dictator, they'd laugh their heads off. Absolutely no one would believe her. It was too hokey, too fairy taleish for words. But the reality was so much more than she could ever have imagined. It was wonderful and magical and made her reassess everything she'd ever believed about Cinderella and Snow White and all the other fairy-tale love stories she'd ever heard. Maybe there *was* an element of truth to them after all!

"Nick," she murmured, unable to keep a smile off her face, "I sincerely hope you enjoyed that half as much as I did."

He laughed and gathered her close. He dropped a kiss into her hair. "I enjoyed you twice as much. You are a miracle, my darling."

The depth of feeling in his voice was real. Katy's spirits soared, her bubbling ecstasy finally set free. She threw her arms around his neck and kissed him soundly on the mouth. "You're the amazing one, Nick Ramsey."

His exultant laughter mingled with hers as they shared a leisurely kiss.

She lurched as a quiet knock sounded on the door. "Please, ma'am, you must go now. Your companion, he asks for you."

The prison's walls slammed back in around them. Nick pulled her down on top of him for one last quick hug and then he jumped up.

"Coming, Riki," Katy mumbled.

The lock began to rattle, and she fumbled with her clothes, clumsy in her haste to don them again. Nick threw on his pants and shirt and helped her. He was just tucking her face scarf in place when the door creaked open. His laughing gaze met her panicked one.

She scowled and shook her finger at him as she swept toward the door. Out of sight of the young guard, he grabbed her wagging finger and placed a quick kiss on her fingertip. Katy yanked her hand away, smiling widely.

She followed the young prison guard down the

gloomy hall toward the exit, dazed by her abrupt return to the real world. She squinted as she stepped out into the glare of sunset directly on her face.

"Where in the hell have you been?" Larry Grayson growled. "I was about to send in troops after you."

"Long story," she murmured as they walked past a dozen or more Army soldiers.

They passed through the outer wall of the palace and headed down the hill toward their hotel. She thought fast while they walked. She needed to come up with a good cover story for spending so much time with Nick. A story that would let her go back and do the same again.

She stopped just in front of the hotel, placing a restraining hand on her partner's arm.

Larry looked at her expectantly. "What gives, Katy?"

She looked around and saw no Army uniforms. She leaned close to him to talk under her breath. "One of the prisoners has become an informal spokesman for the rest. He gathers reports on how everyone's being treated…the kind of stuff the prisoners won't talk to us about with a guard listening right outside their door. I've been talking to him about what's really going on." The lie tasted awful on her tongue, but she had no choice. Extraordinary situations called for extraordinary measures.

Larry's eyes lit up with interest. "Really? Are you finding out things InterAid needs to know about?"

She nodded conspiratorially and embellished her tale even more. "He's working on getting me the names of all the guards who are violating the Geneva Convention protocols. The prisoners are hesitant to complain themselves for fear of reprisals."

Larry nodded. "Of course. Maybe I should take over visiting this guy if he's got this much information."

Alarm sliced through Katy. "No! He wouldn't talk to you. He's just now coming to trust me."

Larry looked skeptical. "You don't have the experience to do something like this. The information you gather may well end up in an international court of law, and you have to know what you're doing to collect it impartially so you don't compromise its worth as testimony."

Katy's alarm escalated into desperation. "I'm telling you, Larry. He won't talk to you. We won't get anything at all unless I continue seeing him."

Larry looked unconvinced.

"Besides, if you start spending lots of time with him, as well, that'll draw way too much attention to him. We'll put him at risk of being discovered and then we'll lose our source altogether."

A disgruntled look settled on her partner's face. "Damn. I suppose you're right."

Katy sighed in relief. "Tell you what, Larry. Once I get the names of the guards and the specifics of what's going on, would you be willing to help me put it all together into an organized format to show to Don Ford?"

His expression cleared. "Absolutely. My pleasure. You know, I'm quite experienced at this kind of thing. In Kosovo, something similar happened to me...."

She restrained a laugh. Somehow she doubted a Slavic prince had asked Larry to secretly marry him and have his baby. Katy stepped inside with him, nodding dutifully in response to the war story he launched into.

Although her ploy bought her the chance to continue seeing Nick, it also brought her unwanted attention from Larry Grayson. He nodded significantly at her the next day as she headed for Nick's cell, and the surly guard caught the look. He frowned, looking back and forth between the two of them.

Crud. Now the guard was suspicious, too. She had to distract him. She racked her brain for an idea. As he wrestled with the huge rusted lock, she murmured to the guard, "Sheesh. These American men. So forward with women. Give me an Arab man anytime over one of those gorillas."

The guard looked up at her in surprise. He looked back over his shoulder at Larry Grayson's retreating back.

He grinned wolfishly and growled, "Want me to kill him for insulting your honor?"

Katy lurched. "Uh, no. That's okay. But thank you for the offer. I'll let you know if he ever truly insults my honor."

The guard nodded conspiratorially and patted the pistol at his side. "Say the word and I'll blow his head off."

Katy blinked and did her best to smile back at the goon. "Uh, thanks."

What was she turning into? She was lying to everyone she met these days. First the Baraqi woman, then Larry and now the prison guard. She slipped into Nick's cell. And all of a sudden the lies were worth it. He took her breath away just to look at him.

He was standing on the far side of his cell, looking up the air shaft, apparently. The door closed and he turned. She pulled off her veil.

In three swift strides he crossed the cell. Their bodies met and they kissed greedily. His tongue swept inside her mouth the same way his presence swept inside her heart, in a rush of heat and passion. He picked her up in his arms and spun her around slowly, kissing her all the while.

"I missed you," he murmured.

She smiled back. "I missed you, too."

He reached beneath her robe and pushed it off her shoulders. Nick smiled at her vibrant yellow dress. "Rebelling against the dress code, are we?" he murmured.

She laughed up into his warm gaze. "I thought you might enjoy a ray of sunshine in this gray prison."

"Aah, my darling, you are all the light and warmth I need."

"We don't have much time," she whispered. "The nasty guard's on shift. Plus, my partner's been asking some questions. He's noticed how much time I'm spending with you."

Nick reached down, pulling up the hem of her loose sleeveless sundress. He backed her against the wall, kissing and sucking at her breasts through the dress and her bra until she moaned in abandon.

"What explanation did you give your partner?" Nick asked as his hands divested her of her panties and began to play their magic on her already throbbing flesh.

"I, uh…" Her knees went weak and she clutched at Nick's powerful biceps. "Uh, told him you had information about guards violating…" Her breath failed her as he knelt before her and his mouth closed upon the most sensitive parts of her.

"Uh, violating, uh… Oh, my…the Geneva Conventions."

"Mmm," Nick murmured. "Clever. I'll see if I can find out anything for you."

He rose to his full height before her, his gaze an inferno of desire that matched the ferocity of the one blazing inside her. He fumbled at his own clothes for a second and then his arms went around her.

"I can't get enough of you," he growled as he backed her up against the wall again.

He lifted her, and Katy's legs wrapped around his waist. He settled her down onto his heated flesh, and she gasped at the pulsing fullness within her.

The wall was cold at her back: Nick was answering fire before her. She clung to his broad shoulders, riding the storm between them as it grew wilder and more powerful, surging within her, until finally it tore her completely apart and scattered her before its fury.

She collapsed against Nick's muscular chest, breathing hard.

He buried his face against her neck, laughing quietly. "I haven't been this crazy over a woman since I was seventeen and in love for the first time."

Katy hugged him close. "Was she beautiful?"

"Who?" Nick asked.

"The woman you were in love with."

He grinned down at her as he eased her onto her feet but continued to hold her close. "Indubitably. She was also about twenty years older than me. It turns out she took great pleasure in initiating young men into the ways of love."

Katy smiled up at him. "Then I guess I owe her a thanks someday if I ever meet her."

He returned her smile. "No, sweet Katy. You owe her nothing. There has never been another woman who does to me what you do. You drive me out of my mind. What we have between us is not about technique. It's about passion and generosity and love."

Katy stared. "Love?"

The smile faded from his amber eyes, leaving them glowing like quiet embers. "Yes, Katy. I feel like I have known you for a lifetime. You have opened my heart and filled it with your spirit. You have made me happy."

"How can you be happy? You're about to die!" As soon as she blurted out the words, she wished them back. "Oh! I'm so sorry—"

Nick laid a finger over her lips. "No need to apologize. You speak the truth. Never be afraid to do that with me."

"But—"

He stopped her again. "But nothing. You don't owe me any response to my, er, declaration. I don't expect you to return my feelings in so short a time. Maybe I feel this way so soon because I *am* about to die. But that doesn't make the feelings any less real for now."

Katy looked into her heart. Did she honestly care why he loved her? It didn't matter, really. If falling in love with her was his mind's way of distracting him from the horrors awaiting him, so be it. She could live with that. Scary thing was, she had a sneaking suspicion that she did return his feelings, at least to some degree. He was handsome, romantic and oh so tragic. Prince Charming, indeed. How could a girl not love him just a little?

Of course, the whole idea of truly being in love with Nick was ridiculous. That desperate, giddy hunger she felt every moment they were apart was just infatuation, and it was most certainly intensified by the drama of the situation. Nonetheless, it hit her like a semitruck every time she left him. No doubt about it—she was dangerously close to being in love with him, too.

He continued, "I know it sounds absurd. But I'm not some teenage kid anymore who thinks the first big crush that comes along is true love. Hell, I've been in and out of more relationships than I care to count."

He pushed a strand of hair back from her brow and gazed down at her earnestly. "Maybe because my death is near, I'm more aware of what a privilege it is to be alive. I'm more aware of my feelings. Of the people around me. These few extra days I've been given have been unexpectedly enlightening. Thankfully I've learned to really live before I die."

Katy nodded in perfect understanding. Knowing Nick had stripped away everything but the essentials for her, too.

He continued, "It all boils down to living joyfully. To loving with all your heart. To savoring every moment."

Katy reached up to stroke his face where the ugly red of his bruises was turning dark purple and green. "You are an amazing man, Nick Ramsey. To find meaning in life even in your situation…"

"Don't pity me, Katy," he whispered. "Appreciate being alive with me. Share this joy."

Tears filled her eyes as she gazed up at him. The irony

of such words in the mouth of a condemned man tore her heart in two. She flung her arms around his neck, hugging him tightly. She choked out, "No pity. Only joy between us. I promise."

He hugged her so tight she thought they might melt into one person.

A fist banged on the door. "Let's go," the guard called out irritably.

Katy wiped her eyes hastily as Nick retrieved her *abaya* from the floor. He threw it around her shoulders and tucked in her veil for her. Before he stepped back, he wiped away a last tear clinging to her eyelashes and brought his fingertip to his mouth to kiss it off his finger.

The poignancy of the gesture nearly caused her to break down sobbing again.

"Go," he urged.

She touched his cheek and turned to leave.

Nick sagged against the wall as the door shut beside him. He raged and grieved at the four silent stone walls for the time they'd never have together, for the child he'd never know, for all the happiness he was going to miss out on.

And finally, when he had no more anger or pain left, he rejoiced for what they had found with one another. He didn't know if his feelings were real or not, and frankly he didn't care. He was perfectly happy to wallow in the euphoria Katy brought to him instead of dwelling on the inevitable.

After a long time, he pulled himself together and went to the air shaft. There was still a little light left to see by. He retrieved the paper and pen he'd hidden on the ledge outside and began to write.

I, Nikolas Hassan Akeem el Ramsey, being of sound mind and body, do declare the following to be my last will and testament....

He also wrote a separate letter verifying that he had secretly married Katy. It also named any offspring of their relationship as his heir.

His education in banking came in handy for once as he drafted the legal documents. At least he hoped they were legal. They'd no doubt come under challenge when they were revealed to whatever government held Baraq at the time. He did his best to anticipate the loopholes and word them in such a way as to leave no doubt about his sanity or his intentions regarding his wife and possible child.

He read through the drafts in the last remnants of twilight that trickled down to him and made a few changes here and there. In the beginning, his plan had only been about having a baby. But now his concern was also for Katy, to leave her financially secure and able to find happiness on her own terms. Funny how his perspective had changed in so short a time. It was not just about himself and his legacy anymore. Now it was about another human being, too. Apparently old dogs *could* learn new tricks if put under sufficient duress.

Katy was trudging back down into the city after a long day, worn out both physically and emotionally. The smells of dinner cooking swirled out of doorways, and the sounds of everyday life wrapped around her.

It was really hard sometimes to keep up a good front for Nick when every time she saw him she wanted to cry. What a tragedy that the people of Baraq would never come to know him the way she had. Men didn't come any more honorable than him. His courage in the face of his healing nose and fading bruises—and what they represented—was remarkable.

Even if the two of them didn't succeed in creating an heir, she would find a way to tell his story someday, not to let his final gift to the Baraqi people be forgotten.

A hand touched her arm and she jolted in surprise. A veiled woman stood beside her. "Hanah and her friend send their greetings. Could you come with me for a moment?"

Katy blinked, startled. "Uh, sure."

She followed this new woman into a small pharmacy. They strolled down a row of first-aid supplies that was becoming alarmingly depleted. The usual Western brands were conspicuously absent. Was Sharaf outlawing foreign products now, too? What would be next to go? Baby formula?

The woman leaned near to whisper, "We have found a route out. Now we must find a passenger."

Katy turned her head to stare directly at the woman. "You're sure it's safe?"

The woman nodded.

Hope flared in Katy's chest. Was it possible? Was there a way to get Nick out of Baraq alive? At this point, she was willing to entertain any ideas on that subject, no matter how crazy they might be.

"How?" she murmured as she picked up a bottle of

something that might be cough syrup except it was tar-thick and black. What it was, she didn't want to know.

"The how is not important right now. What's vital is that we find him."

Katy caught the gaze of the man behind the front counter upon them. She nodded at her companion and smiled pleasantly as if they were chatting about the weather.

The woman continued, "We know he was in the palace when it fell. He was seen going down. But after that he disappeared. It is believed impossible that he escaped the palace. His last known position was overrun too quickly for that. We believe he may be a prisoner of war."

Katy glanced sideways at the woman and picked up a random box off the shelf. Good grief. It looked like an enema kit. She put it back hastily.

"What do you want from me?" she muttered.

"Check the prisoner records. See if he's among them."

"I can assure you, if Nikolas Ramsey were listed in our records, he'd be long dead by now."

"Then you must search among the prisoners."

"And what do I do if I find him?"

"Tell us. We will do all the rest."

Right. Whoever *we* was. For all she knew, this woman was a spy sent by Sharaf to see what InterAid knew and wasn't telling him. Katy had no way of knowing if this woman was legit or not. The woman could have tossed out a couple names of suspected Ramsey loyalists to throw Katy off and could be, in fact, a hardcore Sharaf supporter.

What a mess. Even if someone wanted to and maybe

even could help Nick, she had no way of distinguishing them from those who wished Nick ill.

She grabbed what she thought was a bottle of aspirin and headed for the checkout with it. The way the proprietor had been eyeing them, she figured she better buy something or else the guy would surely report her to Sharaf's men. And that was the last complication Katy needed right now. Her life was already messy enough.

The man wrapped her purchase in a piece of brown butcher paper and gave her a handful of change. She kept her eyes downcast, as was expected nowadays, as she took her change and mumbled her thanks. Sheesh. What a demeaning way to have to live. It only took a single moment of being forced to act like this to erase any doubts in her mind about the rightness of what she was doing with Nick.

She might have chosen the more dangerous path, the one that led to certain heartbreak. But it was also the path free of regrets and filled with the satisfaction that she hadn't sat by in the face of suffering and injustice and done nothing.

The next two weeks settled into a routine for Nick. He started growing a beard in hopes that it might buy him a day or two. He slept and ate. And he lived in a slow motion of suspended animation until Katy came to him, and then the minutes flew by at light speed until she had to go again. With her InterAid partner's help and the cooperation of the guard Riki, they managed to grab a few extra minutes together here and there. It wasn't nearly enough, but it was sufficient to keep him from going stark raving mad. And hopefully it was enough to have planted a baby in her womb. He chose to believe they had succeeded at that because the alternative was unthinkable.

Katy didn't know how Nick kept from losing his mind. She lived on the ragged edge of losing it herself—and she had plenty of work to keep her busy in the times between her visits with him.

Her life was divided into Nick and everything else. Everything else was a gray fog that she waded through unconsciously until it was time once more to go bask in the bright sunlight of Nick's love for her.

She measured the passage of time by how long it had been since she'd seen Nick and how long it was until she'd see him again. She made mental notes of all the details around her so she could describe them to him. She picked out her clothes with Nick in mind. She brushed her teeth for him. She ate and slept for him. Breathed for him.

He was an addiction in her blood. She knew it was dangerous to be with him. She knew their relationship could get them both killed. She knew it was inevitable that he would be discovered. But none of it mattered. The more she was with him, the more she craved him.

Her feelings for him grew past love. Past obsession. She felt as though she were gradually becoming one with him. When she was away from him, she imagined that she could feel his aches and pains, the hard, cold ledge he slept on, the coolness of water in his throat when he drank.

The guards grew accustomed to her routine, and nobody seemed to question the extra time she spent with Prisoner 1806 each day. Thankfully the veil hid her face when she emerged from his cell. She didn't think she was capable of hiding the ecstasy of making love with him or the agony of leaving him.

It was after one such leave-taking when Katy was surprised to see Don Ford walk up to her in the gloomy corridor, and not Larry.

"Ah, there you are, Katy," he said politely. "The invisible aid worker."

Katy blinked, alarmed. Uh-oh. What did her boss want? She cast back over her reports and forms. She was pretty sure she'd been doing all her work as she was supposed to.

Don took her by the arm and escorted her past the phalanx of guards and out into the city. "Walk with me," he ordered.

They strolled through the bazaar, dodging blankets on the ground with wares spread on them. It smelled of spices, greasy food and animal dung. It was intriguing and repellent at the same time.

"What's going on with you?" Don asked her abruptly.

"What do you mean?" Katy replied carefully. "Is there something wrong with my work?"

"Not at all. Your work's fine. Larry tells me you've forged a relationship with one of the prisoners. How's that going?"

"Fine," she mumbled, begging her face not to blush.

"Learning anything interesting?"

Katy choked. She'd been learning some very interesting things indeed. Nick was nothing if not an inventive lover. Nick had also done as he'd said he would and learned bits and pieces about how the other prisoners were faring. How he did that, she had no idea.

"Uh, the last few interrogations of prisoners have been more violent than usual." Katy glanced around for soldiers before she continued under her breath, "Apparently the regime's having some internal troubles or maybe has gotten wind of something among the prisoners it doesn't like."

Don gave her a sharp look. He leaned over to look at a carved clay pipe and murmured as he passed close to her, "Your contact is right. I don't know what it is, but the Army's got a burr up its—er, they're hot and bothered about something."

Panic flitted in Katy's breast. Oh Lord. What if they'd heard a rumor that Nick was still alive? If random strangers on the street were whispering to her about it, odds were the Army had heard the rumor, too. Could the Army have renewed its search for him? Over the past week that had seemed to die down a bit.

"Do you have any idea what it could be that's got the Army so worked up?" she asked, her heart in her throat.

"None. I was hoping you could tell me."

She never had been able to lie worth a darn. Nonetheless, she gave him her best innocent look, shook her head and hoped he bought it.

Don murmured, "I can tell you this, though." He spoke so quietly she had to turn her ear to his mouth to hear him. "I'm having to jump through hoops and negotiate my butt off to keep the regime from slaughtering the prisoners wholesale. I just spent two hours talking General Sharaf out of it. Again. This is the third time he's declared he's going to kill them all, down to the last man."

Sick dread settled in Katy's stomach. Sharaf knew. The general knew Nick was alive and masquerading as a common soldier among the prisoners. Why else would he abruptly decide to kill them all?

"Did you have any indication the regime would take such a hard line with the prisoners when we first came to Baraq?" she probed.

Don shook his head. "That's what's so strange. They seemed interested in having us here and in establishing themselves as a legitimate and reasonable government. That's why this one-eighty turnabout is so troubling."

Katy stumbled over the edge of a blanket and Don caught her arm, steadying her. He stopped and turned to face her.

"Katy, do you have any idea at all what could have brought about this sudden change of heart in the Army?"

She stared down at the ground, her heart torn in two. If she told Don the truth—that the Army was trying to eliminate Nick—Don could save the other prisoners. But to do so, he'd have to reveal Nick's identity.

Her heart and her conscience wrestled within her, shredding what little composure she had.

She knew what Nick would want her to do. He'd tell her to save his people. He was going to die anyway. It was only a matter of time.

Except she just didn't want his time to be up yet. She wasn't ready to let him go!

Unable to keep her eyes from filling with tears, she replied, "I'll talk to my contact and see what he says. Maybe he's heard something from one of the other prisoners."

Don nodded solemnly. "Thanks. I appreciate it. And Katy?"

She looked up at his blurry face.

"A piece of advice. You're going to get hurt if you get too involved with these prisoners. You've got to pull back emotionally."

As if she could do that!

He continued, "Frankly you're already too involved. I ought to pull you out and send you home right now. But I need what your contact knows."

He scuffed his feet and looked at her candidly. "I'm walking on a razor's edge here. Two thousand men's lives depend on me talking a mob of power-drunk soldiers out of massacring their prisoners. I don't know how much longer I can hold off Sharaf."

"You'll find a way. I know you will." She added desperately, "You have to."

Chapter 8

Katy stood outside Nick's cell door, staring at the ancient wood in dread. Her heart said not to tell him. Her head told her in no uncertain terms to tell him everything. Except if she told Nick the Army wanted to kill all the prisoners to get him, he'd call a guard instantly and reveal who he was.

Telling him the truth was the right thing to do. The honorable thing. The noble thing. But, dammit, she didn't want to be honorable or noble! She wanted Nick to live a few more days. She needed a few more stolen hours in his arms. She hadn't stored up enough memories of him yet to see her through an entire lifetime.

She was being selfish. Worse, she was jeopardizing the lives of two thousand men. She'd met many of them in the course of doing her job. Knew them by name.

Knew about their families, how afraid they were, how badly they just wanted to get out of prison and go home.

The choice was tearing her in two. She wanted to crawl into bed and bury her head beneath a pillow until it all went away.

Riki pushed the door to cell 1806 open while her internal battle raged. Glumly she stepped inside and listened to the door clang shut behind her.

Nick stepped forward with a smile that faded as soon as he looked her in the eyes. "What's wrong?" he demanded.

"Nothing," she mumbled.

"Bull."

She froze. Busted.

But he let her off the hook. He leaned back and looked down at her fondly. "Have I told you today that I love you and you're beautiful?"

She smiled in spite of herself. "You haven't and I'm not."

"I do and you are. I love your smile."

She gazed back at him sadly. "I love your smile, too. And your eyes. And your heart. And your sense of humor. And your honor...."

Fortunately he didn't seem to notice the way her voice caught on that one. He led her over to the ledge and urged her to sit upon it. He knelt, took off her shoes and socks and commenced rubbing her feet.

"Relax, darling," he murmured.

She groaned in pleasure as the heel of his hand dug into the arch of her foot. His hands drifted higher, to her ankle and lower calf, kneading away a long day spent mostly on her feet. Inch by inch, he moved higher, gradually melting away every last bit of tension in her body. At some point he invited her to lie down on her stomach and he proceeded to give her the most amazing back rub she'd ever experienced. She was completely boneless by the time he finished.

She rolled over on her back to gaze up at him. The bruises on his face were fading to yellow. Like leaves on the trees, the changing colors marked the coming end of their brief summer together. She knew the swelling of his nose under the bandage to be almost gone. Once the black eyes went away, he'd look almost like his normal, gorgeous self again. And then someone would realize who he was.

"Are you displeased with what you see?"

She blinked. "Are you kidding? If you weren't a king you could be a male supermodel. You're turning into one of the most handsome men I've ever seen."

"Aah. And that's the problem. I'm starting to look like myself again. Thank you for the compliment, by the way."

She reached up to stroke his cheekbone above the short beard covering his jaw. He wasn't shaving in hopes that the beard might buy him another few days. "You're such a good person," she murmured.

"Me? Until the last few weeks, my greatest accomplishments in life have been the scoreboard of fast women and fast cars I've collected and crashed. I've done a whole lot of things I'm not proud of and very few I am proud of."

"Maybe, but in the end you did the right thing. You came home when your father died and you took up your responsibility."

He laughed with scant humor. "Yeah, and look where *that* landed me."

"Oh, Nick," she cried out softly. "If only we had more time together. It's just not fair!"

He gazed down at her, wisdom far beyond his years glowing in his golden eyes. "Life is rarely fair, my love. You just have to take what comes and make the best of it."

"And what's the best thing for you? For us? Is it right that you're going to die because of who your father was? You never even got a chance to be king. If you were a despot and oppressed your people, a coup would be one thing. But you're not like that at all. It makes no sense for you to die."

Nick rolled to his side and gathered her close in his arms. "You'll drive yourself mad if you try to make sense of this, Katy. Nothing about this situation is sensible. We just have to accept what is."

"Why? What if you found another way to disguise yourself? There are people outside these walls trying desperately to find you so they can help you escape. Let me contact them and tell them you're alive."

"No!" he said sharply. "You must not tell anyone I am here."

"Why not?" she retorted. "Let me help you live."

"I will not run away from the situation again. If and when the Army recognizes me, I will stand up and take my fate like a man."

Dear God. Was she responsible for his determination to die? If she'd turned him down, said no to his outrageous proposal, would he have fought to preserve the Ramsey line by finding a way to survive this ordeal?

"Dammit, Nick. This isn't about being a man. It's not about proving how brave and noble you are or punishing yourself for your past by letting them kill you. It's about surviving!"

Jaw set, he responded with stony silence. But she wasn't ready to give up yet. She flung more words against the stubborn fortress he'd built around himself.

"What if you become Akbar for real? What if, when the Army eventually releases the prisoners, you just disappear? You could come to the United States and start a new life. With me. Don't you want that? Has everything between us been a sham?" Her voice broke.

He put his hand on the back of her head and pulled her close, absorbing her sobs into his shoulder.

"Sweet Katy. If I were a regular man, I'd love nothing more than to disappear with you and live out the rest of our days quietly. But the fact remains that I am not just any man. I am the king of Baraq. I was born to this fate."

"Bull," she threw back at him. "Fate is what you make of it. You can walk away from being the king. Stop being Nick Ramsey and be someone else. My government sets up new identities for people all the time. Plastic surgeons can make you look completely different. Nobody will ever find you."

"But I will still be me. Even if I did change my name and appearance, in my heart—in my soul—I would still be me. I would still owe a duty to this country and I would still feel responsible for my people. As tempting an offer as you make, I could not live with myself if I ran away from doing the right thing."

"How can it be the right thing to die?" she cried.

"You're an American. You, of all people, should understand. Your country was founded upon the blood of men and women who were willing to die for a principle. Your countrymen still die today for that same principle."

"We're not talking about democracy here. We're talking about your life, Nick!"

He smoothed her tangled hair away from her tear-streaked face. "My love, we're talking about what it means to be a king. I allowed Kareem to talk me into hiding among the soldiers once. And I'm glad he did or else I never would have found you. Not only have you given me a chance to preserve the Ramsey name, but you've taught me more about life and love in these few days than I learned in a lifetime before you."

His gaze pierced straight to her soul. "But make no mistake—I will not run again. Next time I will die like a king."

Panic clawed at Katy, ripping the flesh from her bones, gashing her heart until her lifeblood gushed away. She placed her hands on both sides of Nick's face and looked deeply into his sorrowful, implacable eyes.

"Nick. Do this for me. Please. I'm begging you. Live. For me. Put aside your duty, your guilt, your overgrown sense of responsibility."

He shook his head and started to speak, but she cut him off. "Don't you understand? I can't live without you!"

"I promise to give you the sun and the moon and the stars in my heart before I die, Katy. But the one thing I cannot give you is happily ever after."

She drew breath to argue, but instead a knock sounded upon the door.

"Miss Katy," Riki murmured urgently through the panel. "I must ask you to go now. My commander comes this way."

Katy jumped to her feet and frantically threw on her veil. As she slipped out the door, she paused just long enough to whisper, "Please, Nick."

Katy tossed and turned all night. Her sheets grew hot and tangled, and finally she got up in the wee hours of the morning to take a cool bath. What was she going to do if Nick didn't see reason?

She even considered calling the U.S. government back in Washington to ask for help in pulling Nick out. Maybe the State department could bully Sharaf into handing him over to the Americans. But would he go? She doubted it. Knowing him, he'd make a grand gesture and insist on staying right where he was, receiving the same treatment as the common soldiers.

God, he was frustrating! What was so wrong with happily ever after? She felt like tearing her hair out and screaming at his obstinate attitude. While she understood his point of view in principle, it was also suicidal. Why couldn't he see that his nation needed him? Not his child, not a vague hope of a restored Ramsey throne. *Him.*

Once the Baraqi people got to know him as well as she did, they'd adore him. He'd lead his country brilliantly out of its economic and social troubles and into prosperity. She had no doubt whatsoever about that.

She went back to bed after her bath, but still sleep evaded her.

In the morning she dragged herself downstairs for breakfast with the other InterAid workers. Unfortunately her distress was such that the mere thought of food made her ill. She choked down a few grapes and a hunk of dry flatbread.

This morning she and Larry were visiting another Army installation outside of Akuba. Several dozen prisoners had just been transferred to the facility, and they were to check on the men's status.

As they stepped into the makeshift prison, Katy noticed right away that something was afoot with this bunch of prisoners. They were badly, even brutally, beaten. In fact, she spent much of the morning taking Polaroid pictures for the complaint that she and Larry would be filing regarding the treatment of this batch of prisoners.

And then, as she tended their wounds and started talking to them, a horrifying pattern began to take shape. All these men were from the palace guard. And they'd all been questioned—ruthlessly—about where the king had disappeared to on the night of the coup.

It was all Katy could do to continue rendering aid to them. Each bruise, each cigarette burn, each broken bone was *her fault.* If she'd told Nick yesterday that the Army was looking for him, as she should have, none of these men would have been beaten and tortured last night. Guilt forced the little breakfast she'd eaten back into her throat time and time again.

Her hands shook so badly she could barely write the notes Larry dictated to her as he sutured wounds, put arms back into sockets and set bones as best he could without anesthesia.

Finally they'd seen every prisoner. Larry lectured the Army officer in charge forcefully about proper prisoner treatment while she looked on, and the two of them were duly thrown out of the jail.

Larry rubbed his hands over his face. "Lord, that was a mess. You held up great, Katy."

She laughed shakily. "I faked it."

He looked sharply at her. "You look like hell. Why don't you go back to the hotel and call it a day? I'll do your rounds at the palace for you."

"No, that's okay. There's someone I have to talk to."

"Your contact?" he asked astutely.

"Yeah," she answered glumly.

"Tell him any help he can give us will be greatly appreciated. They're not the first palace guards we've run into who've been treated like that."

"Really?" Katy hadn't heard about any other incidents. But then, she rarely spent time with the other members of the team. She spent every moment she could with Nick and then had to work extra to make up the lost time. By the time she got back to the hotel each night, she was too exhausted to do anything but gulp down a bite to eat and head for bed.

Larry murmured under his breath as they walked down the crowded street, "A couple of our guys ran into a batch of prisoners yesterday who were so messed up most of them couldn't even sit up. The way I hear it, they went through Vietnam-style torture. Broken backs, amputated fingers, pulled teeth—the works. We're filing a big complaint over it."

Katy lurched to a stop, her hand over her mouth. She

looked around frantically and tore off her facial veil. She bent over the curb and threw up the entire meager contents of her stomach.

Larry's hand landed on her shoulder. "Jeez, Katy. I'm sorry. Didn't realize you were touchy about stuff like that. I figured with you being who you are and all, you were used to hearing about gory stuff."

She wiped her mouth on her cuff. The bitter taste of gall nearly made her ill again. "My brothers don't talk about their cases over the dinner table," she choked out.

"Come on back to the hotel. Let's get a decent meal in you. I've got some stuff that'll calm your stomach."

"No," she managed to force past her clenched teeth. "I'll be okay. You just surprised me."

"You've been losing a lot of weight, Katy. You've got to take care of yourself, you know. What we do takes a toll on a person."

He had no idea the toll it was taking on her. "Thanks for your concern, Larry. But, really, I'll be okay. Let's just go to the palace so I can—" She broke off.

"Yeah, I know. So you can put the screws to your contact and tell him to get cracking and get us solid evidence so we can put a halt to all this crap."

"Something like that," she managed to force out.

The smells of the bazaar almost made Katy sick again, but she managed to stagger through the squalor to the palace. She waited impatiently while the guards completed a shift change, but finally Riki led her down the dark corridor of cells. It was so dark that when she drew even with the door to Nick's cell, it took her a second to notice that it stood open a few inches.

"Riki, what's going on here?" she asked. "This prisoner's door isn't locked!"

Oh, God. Something had happened to Nick. He was so hurt he couldn't move, and they hadn't bothered locking him in.

She shoved open the heavy door and rushed inside. And stopped cold. He wasn't standing at the window as he usually did. Nor was he lying on his hard ledge. He wasn't in the cell at all.

She whirled, barely able to breathe. "Riki," she gasped, "where did they take him? What's happened to him?"

The young guard shrugged, and she leaped forward, grabbing his shirt in her desperation. "You have to tell me!"

The young man looked genuinely alarmed. "Miss Katy, I don't know. I just came on duty."

She realized she was clutching his shirt in her fists and she forced her fingers to let go.

She whispered, because her only alternative was to scream, "Please, you must help me! I have to find this prisoner. I have to know what's happened to him!"

Chapter 9

Katy followed Riki back out to the guard room, her heart pounding. She kept her eyes downcast—lest she reveal her panic—while he asked his fellow guards about the missing soldier. But nobody seemed to know or care what had happened to Prisoner 1806.

What is going on?

She dragged the reluctant teen to his commander's office and all but pushed the lad through the door. Major Moubayed stepped outside a moment later. He looked annoyed that a foreign infidel, and a woman at that, was pestering him. But Katy didn't much care at the moment.

Katy spoke without waiting to be spoken to. Another faux pas, but tough. "What have you done with Prisoner 1806? We were not notified that you were going to move him," she said as rationally as she could manage.

"We are not required to notify you of anything we do with our prisoners," Moubayed informed her curtly.

"That may be true, but I am required to report on the status of each prisoner I'm tracking." She added in the nicest voice she could muster, "Please, sir, if you could just tell me what you've done with him?"

The officer gave her a disgusted look. "One moment." He stepped back into his office.

Katy started when a hand touched her shoulder. Arab men never touched strange women. She whirled, alarmed.

It was Larry Grayson. "What's up?"

"They've moved one of the prisoners."

"They move prisoners all the time," he said, confused.

She stared at him significantly until she saw the light-bulb go on in his brain. They'd moved *that* prisoner.

Moubayed stepped out of his office again. As soon as he saw Larry, he turned his back on Katy as if she didn't exist. "Aah, Mr. Grayson. You have saved me the trouble of finding you. Come with me."

Larry didn't move. "Where are we going?" he asked suspiciously.

Katy stopped in the act of following the soldier, surprised by Larry's obvious reluctance. What did he know that she didn't?

"You will come with me," Moubayed ordered imperiously.

"No, we will not," Larry answered politely but just as firmly.

The officer spoke in rapid Arabic and several soldiers stepped forward. One of them poked Katy in the back with a rifle, and two others grabbed Larry by his arms.

She froze in place, too shocked to move.

"Don't resist them," Larry murmured in English.

"Silence!" Moubayed barked.

Katy stumbled as she was shoved again from behind. Oh, God. What had she done? What had she gotten them into?

They walked upstairs into the palace proper, into the royal apartments. It was the first time Katy had ever been in this part of the edifice. It must have been beautiful before the coup ruined so much of its decor.

As they were shoved into the wrecked remains of a gorgeous room, Larry maneuvered close enough to her to murmur, "Let me do the talking."

The room was long and narrow, with a high ceiling and colonnaded walls lined with tall stained-glass windows. Sunlight streamed through the cut glass, pouring rainbows of color across the white marble floors. Broken wires dangling from the ceiling announced where a chandelier must have hung until recently. A few of the windows were clumsily boarded over, as well. At the far end of the room she glimpsed a large carved chair encrusted in colored stones—probably real jewels, if the opulence of the rest of the room was any indication. The Ramsey crest—crossed swords flanked by a pair of lions—was carved into the wall and decorated with real swords behind the elaborate chair.

This must be the throne room.

Except now it was lined with tables and desks, and twenty or more Army officers of varying ranks and ages worked on the assorted computers and phones.

Katy followed Larry down the impressive length of the room toward the throne. *Nick's throne.* At the last second, their guards veered off and shoved them toward an inconspicuous door tucked behind the throne. A guard stationed beside the door opened it for them. The panel swung back to reveal a small but opulent sitting room. It, too, had been converted into a utilitarian office.

A handsome man—Katy guessed him to be maybe fifty years old—stepped out from behind the desk and said in French, "I am General Nagheb. I understand you've been making a big stink over one of our prisoners."

Katy drew breath to answer, but Larry sent her a quelling look.

"I wouldn't call it a stink at all, sir," the American answered smoothly. "We merely asked about the status of a prisoner who was moved sometime between yesterday afternoon and now. I'm sure there's been a misunderstanding of some kind."

"No misunderstanding," the general growled. "You were asking about Prisoner 1806."

Larry shrugged. "I think that was the number. I'd have to check my list."

"Don't play games with me!" the general snapped.

Katy recoiled at the harshness of his tone. A rifle poked her in the back, silently ordering her to be still.

Larry was immediately apologetic. "I'm sorry. You are right—this is no game. It is very serious business indeed. InterAid has been charged with full and detailed observation of prisoner treatment in Baraq. We're merely attempting to do our job as stated by your commanders. No more, I assure you."

Katy gulped. She'd done, oh, a teensy bit more than that. Thank God a veil hid her face right now.

With a sharp hand gesture, the general waved all the soldiers out of the office. He glared at Katy and Larry in silence until the door closed behind the last man.

General Nagheb turned to them, his face abruptly calm and his expression pleasant. The transformation was startling. He asked quietly in flawless English, "What do you know about Prisoner 1806?"

Larry blinked in surprise and answered, "Mr. Mulwami has become an informal leader among the prisoners. He keeps abreast of what's going on among the others and has been helpful to us in our efforts to monitor how the prisoners are being treated."

Katy stared at Larry, appalled. What was he doing? He was handing Nick to this guy on a silver platter!

The general nodded. "Go on."

Larry continued blithely, "He has hinted to us that there may have been violations of the Geneva Conventions against the prisoners, particularly in interrogations."

Katy balled her hands into fists. She doubted she'd be allowed to throttle her partner, but she was tempted to give it a try. Why not just lay Nick's head on the chopping block for him?

Larry's voice abruptly changed tone, became much more forceful. "Hence, our particular interest when this prisoner abruptly disappears. InterAid will strenuously object if any reprisals are forthcoming against Mr. Mulwami for his assistance to us with our work."

Katy subsided. Aah. Larry was attempting to put the muscle of InterAid behind protecting Nick. It might be a small, private organization, but it had the ear of some big dogs in Washington. And surely this general knew that.

"Furthermore—" Larry gathered a head of steam "—my partner and I don't appreciate being bullied around at gunpoint. We are honored guests in your country and such treatment is wholly unacceptable."

The general smiled, acknowledging Larry's tactic in invoking the Islamic law of hospitality by declaring himself a guest in Baraq. Then the man said blandly, "I apologize if my subordinates were overenthusiastic in carrying out their orders to bring you to me immediately."

Larry nodded politely, but Katy's attention swiveled completely to the general at his next words.

"Prisoner 1806 has been lying to us about his identity. He is not Akbar Mulwami, as he has claimed."

It felt as though a sledgehammer had just hit her squarely in the gut. The air whooshed out of her lungs, and it was all she could do to hang on to consciousness.

They'd found him.

Nick stared out the window. His eyes hurt, unaccustomed to the brightness of direct sunlight. He didn't care, though. He was so grateful to see the light of day, to feel its warmth upon his skin, that he didn't mind the pain.

They'd found him.

It hadn't been nearly as dramatic or violent as he'd anticipated. The door of his cell had opened and an Army general he'd never seen before had stepped inside.

"My name is George Nagheb," the man had said quietly.

Nick had recognized the name as belonging to the Army's chief of intelligence. He'd never gotten a chance to meet the man in the short time he'd been back in Baraq. He'd heard that Nagheb was brilliant and highly educated. A shame he'd never gotten to work with the man, maybe forge an alliance, maybe share a goal of restoring Baraq to its former glory.

The general had bowed briefly and said simply, "Your Highness, if you would please come with me?"

And that was that. There'd been no questions, no need for denials, no decision of whether or not to confess and be done with it or to try to buy a little more time.

Actually, he was relieved. He'd worried that when the moment came, he wouldn't pull off his surrender with the dignity required of a king. Whatever else happened, Nick was grateful to Nagheb for that.

So far they hadn't questioned him at all. They'd just put him in his father's bedroom with several silent, watchful guards outside the door. At first he'd been confused about why they'd brought him here. And then he'd realized that these were the king's quarters. His quarters now.

Except he'd been too busy to move into them before the coup happened. Not to mention the idea of moving into his father's rooms felt weird. During the one week he'd been king, he'd resided in the chambers he'd grown up in.

He looked around his father's private sitting room. Oddly enough, the place hadn't been looted. Priceless paintings still hung on the walls, and fabulously expensive knickknacks still sat on the tables.

He turned back to the window and his thoughts. He could just imagine the chaos that news of his discovery was causing at Army headquarters. It brought a sardonic smile to Nick's lips. He might have lost the war, but he savored the small victory of surprising them.

It was all he had left.

Katy had known this moment would come. She'd tried to steel herself to face it, but nothing could've prepared her for the shock of the actual event.

Larry stuttered, "He isn't? Then who is he?"

Katy looked away hastily as Larry's gaze swung questioningly toward her. He would see the lie in her eyes. He'd see that she'd known all along who Nick was.

The general's voice came as from a great distance. "Miss McMann, why don't you tell your partner who Prisoner 1806 actually is."

She looked up at the general in shock. They knew about her relationship with Nick, too? Good Lord. Then she was sunk, as well. If they executed her, too, then any chance for the Ramsey line to continue would be lost. She *had* to stay alive, for Nick's sake.

Her voice steadier than she'd have believed possible, she looked General Nagheb directly in the eye. "I have no idea who Prisoner 1806 is. I knew him only as Akbar Mulwami. I recall he showed me his passport when I first spoke to him."

Even to her ears, the lie sounded convincing. Funny how desperation gave her the strength to say that. She prayed Nagheb bought it. The general stared at her for several long seconds, her words hanging in the air between them. Finally he looked away, apparently accepting her answer. Katy let out the breath she'd been holding. Light-headedness washed over her.

General Nagheb glanced at his office door and then said quietly, "Prisoner 1806 is His Royal Highness, King Nikolas Ramsey of Baraq."

Larry jolted beside Katy, and belatedly she remembered to act surprised, as well. Yet again she was grateful for the *abaya* and veil that hid her ineptitude as an actress.

"You're kidding!" Larry exclaimed.

The general walked behind his desk and sat. He pushed several photos toward Larry. "Do you recognize this man?"

Katy looked over her partner's shoulder at several glossy official photographs of Nick decked out in a gaudy military uniform, a crown on his head. His face was in one piece in these photos, but there was no mistaking him. Lord, he was gorgeous.

"Is this the same man you know as Prisoner 1806?"

Larry frowned and picked up a picture to stare at it more closely. "I've only seen Prisoner 1806 once. He had a broken nose and a lot of facial bruising and swelling. I couldn't tell you if they're the same man or not."

He turned to Katy. "You see him all the time. Are they the same guy?"

She stared at the picture Larry shoved into her hands. Her belly twisted in a knot at the idea of identifying Nick. For so long she'd worked not to reveal the truth, there was no way she could bring herself to do it now.

She answered reluctantly, "If Prisoner 1806's face were fully healed, they would definitely look a lot alike. But I couldn't say for sure that they're the same man."

The general leaned back in his chair and stared speculatively at her.

Finally he remarked, "Your identification of the king is not necessary. He has admitted his identity already."

Katy's stomach dropped to her feet. She couldn't have drawn in a breath at that moment if her life depended on it.

It was over.

Nick had turned himself in after all.

Tears surged into her eyes, and she fought them off furiously. *Her* life might very well depend on not falling apart for the next several minutes. Finally fear conquered her grief. She stood ramrod-stiff, praying that the general would let them go so she could go back to her hotel room and die.

The general was speaking again. "And as you know, the Geneva Conventions require certain standards of treatment for heads of state and other dignitaries. These have been provided to His Highness."

Larry's voice replied, barely audible through her agony, "Of course, you understand that we will need to verify this."

"Of course."

What were they talking about? Why wouldn't they just shut up so she could get out of here? Her muscles ached from the strain of holding her body upright.

"You won't mind, then, if we visit King Nikolas? Now, perhaps?"

Katy's attention snapped to Larry. See Nick? Now? Her heart began beating once more.

The general's piercing, far-too-intelligent gaze turned on her. "That can be arranged. A moment, please."

Katy quivered in anticipation, while circulation returned to her limbs and her fingers regained feeling. She watched the general closely as he spoke quickly into a phone, wishing desperately that she spoke better Arabic.

General Nagheb hung up. "You may send one InterAid representative to see the prisoner. One only."

Larry nodded his thanks. "Since Miss McMann has been this prisoner's case worker all along, I'd prefer that she see him. It gives our records better continuity if the same person makes all the entries."

Katy couldn't believe her luck, nor that Larry had stepped aside this time. A second door to the room opened and a guard stepped in. General Nagheb instructed the soldier in French to take Katy to see the king. She squeezed Larry's hand briefly as she passed by him, the gesture buried in a fold of her *abaya* as she swept past. His eyes smiled in return. If only he knew just what a gift he'd given both her and Nick. Maybe someday she could tell him.

"I'll wait for you and escort you back to the hotel," Larry called after her as she rushed out of the room and toward Nick.

The soldier led her down a maze of long hallways, each more gorgeous than the last. The architecture of the palace was stunning, especially given how old a structure it was. Despite the heavy exterior walls, the place felt light and airy inside, uncluttered. Breathtaking frescoes covered the ceilings, and light poured through banks of well-placed windows facing the interior courtyards of the palace.

And then the guard stopped at an ornate set of double doors guarded by several heavily armed soldiers. There was a brief exchange in Arabic, and then each of the soldiers grabbed a door and pushed it open. The splendor of the room in front of her made everything she'd seen so far in this elegant palace pale by comparison.

"You may go in," her escort said.

He made as if to follow her, and she stopped. "It is customary that InterAid interviews prisoners without guards present. That way the prisoners feel comfortable speaking candidly. I will knock on these doors when I am finished with my interview and am ready to leave."

She'd tried to imbue her voice with the same authority Larry had used earlier.

Apparently it had worked, because her escort bowed his head briefly. "As you wish."

"This may take some time," Katy warned. "This prisoner's change in status requires a great deal of detailed paperwork and new reporting. You know how bureaucracies are." She rolled her eyes as if dreading the job, hoping to take the sting out of her pushiness.

The guard rolled his eyes in return.

Katy turned and stepped into the room. She stopped on the threshold, taking in the spectacular chamber as the doors closed silently behind her. And then she caught sight of Nick standing by a window at the far side of the spacious room, looking pensively out a window. Everything else disappeared but him.

Her gaze locked on his back as she moved toward him. The regal strength of his bearing, even when he thought he was alone, made her want to cry. The senseless tragedy of killing this noble man struck her anew, and finally the tears she'd been holding back so desperately came.

Nick looked out the window at the ruined gardens and thought about his mother. Thank goodness she would never see her rose beds in such condition, particularly at the hands of a country she'd despised. Will she mourn my death? He'd barely seen her since she'd taken him to England at the age of nine, deposited him in a posh boarding school and never looked back. She'd left everything and everyone that had to do with Baraq in her past.

He'd gotten beyond his anger and hurt long ago. Although the professionals told him it was probably why he'd had so much trouble committing to a woman. Something to do with fear of abandonment. At least he wouldn't have to worry about that anymore.

A swish of fabric sounded behind him, and he turned, startled.

Katy!

He stepped forward rapidly, looking over her shoulder for guards. She was alone. Merciful God, he'd expected never to see her again.

Nick wrapped her in a crushing embrace. Relief flooded through him, and he offered up a prayer of thanks.

"You found me," he whispered. "How?"

"Long story," she mumbled against his chest, her voice wobbly.

He felt wetness begin to soak through his shirt. He lifted her chin to look into her watery eyes, to lend her some of his resolve. Now wasn't the time to grieve. Not yet. He needed her to be strong for him for just a little while longer.

"Why the tears? I'm still alive. You promised not to cry until after I'm gone," he teased gently.

She sniffed and tried to smile. "I thought you were gone when I got to your cell and you weren't there."

He led her over to a soft leather sofa and sat, pulling her onto his lap. "Tell me about it."

She relayed quickly the events that had brought her to his side.

"So the guards aren't going to interrupt us until you tell them to?" Nick asked at the end of her recitation.

"That's right," she answered.

A slow smile filled him and spilled over onto his face. "Then I have an idea."

She smiled gamely as he pulled them both up to stand and lifted the black fabric of the *abaya* away from her. Today she wore his favorite dress, a nearly ankle-length sleeveless sheath of bright yellow that brought out the roses in her cheeks and the golden highlights in her hair. It was odd to see her in the bright light of the room's chandelier, with its hundreds of tiny bulbs. He was used to squinting in near-total darkness to make out her features. Now even the slightest nuance of her expression was visible. He drank in the shifting of her thoughts as they danced across her expressive face.

"You need to eat, my love," he murmured. "You're losing weight."

Seen in good light, her face had slimmed down, losing its baby softness and leaving behind a grown woman with stunning features. Her cheekbones were high and classic, her nose narrow and refined. Yup, her great bones had come through as he'd thought they would.

He reached out slowly and tugged the rubber band from the bottom of her braid. Gently he teased her hair free of the plait, running his fingers through it until it flowed in a shimmering wave down her back. "I love your hair," he murmured.

"You just like blondes."

He smiled back at her. "I love *your* blond hair. You should always wear it down like this. I can't keep my hands off it."

She reached awkwardly behind her back for the zipper of her dress.

He stepped forward. "Let me." He turned her around and eased the zipper downward. Her back was slender and creamy and disappeared into tantalizing shadows within the dress. He couldn't resist. He bent down and kissed her shoulder, savoring the taste of her skin.

"You steal my breath away," he murmured against her satin flesh.

His mouth drifted downward, following the feminine indentation of her spine. He pushed the soft cotton off her skin, revealing her slowly as he went. When it became an obstacle to his explorations, he hooked his fingers in her bikini underwear and eased it down, as well.

And then she was nude before him, more beautiful than the Venus de Milo herself as she gazed at him, her eyes swimming with desire and adoration. What man could resist a woman who looked at him like that?

He gazed back at her solemnly. "I love you," he breathed.

"I love you, too," she whispered.

He blinked. Exultation shot through him. "You're not just saying that because the end is near?"

A slight frown marred the smoothness of her brow. "Not at all. I'm saying it because I do love you. With all my heart. Can't you tell?"

He smiled, actually a little embarrassed. "Well, I hoped. But I wasn't sure. I thought I might be imagining it because I wanted you to return my feelings."

She laughed up at him. "Silly man. How could I not love you? You're perfect in every way. Except for being stubborn, of course."

He laughed. "I'm far from perfect, my love."

"You're perfect to me," she murmured.

He gathered her close against him, relishing the feel of her body against his. "Your opinion is all that matters," he whispered back.

They stood there for a moment, enjoying the quiet of their embrace.

"So, madam, how are this prisoner's new living conditions? Are they safe, sanitary and secure according to Geneva Convention standards?"

Katy leaned back and grinned up at him. "I'd say these quarters meet the minimum Geneva standards. Barely."

"Glad to hear it. I wouldn't want to get in the way of you doing your job."

As much as they were both trying to keep the mood

light and enjoy the moment, the passage of time weighed upon him. Desperation hovered just below the surface of Nick's mind. He didn't want to die, dammit! But he had no choice. He might not have lived his life like a king, but by God he'd die like one. Regret stabbed through him. He'd have loved to be with Katy for the next seventy years or so.

"There's food on the table, darling. Are you hungry?"

"I am, but I'm not wasting my time with you eating."

Nonetheless, he headed for the buffet that had been laid out for him. Sharaf wasn't missing a trick when it came to rubbing in all that Nick had lost. "Let's make a picnic of it. I'll bring a platter over to the bed."

She glanced down in dismay at the gorgeous brocade bedspread with the Ramsey lions embroidered on it in gold thread. "But—"

He set the platter on the bed, flopped down beside it and laughed aloud. "What will they do to me if we make a mess? Kill me?" His laughter grew and he couldn't help it. He laughed harder and harder until even he could hear the note of hysteria within it.

And then Katy was there, kneeling over him, holding his face in both her hands. "Look at me, Nick," she ordered. "Stop it!"

He stared up at her, slowly regaining his senses, his laughter dying away.

"I can't imagine what this must be like for you." Then she said more strongly, "But you've got to pull yourself together."

"Why?" he asked fatalistically. "What does it matter? Did you know my execution's set for tomorrow?"

Katy reared back at that, horror painted on her face.

He continued mercilessly. "High noon. Death by hanging. Just like one of your cowboy movies."

Her face crumpled slowly as realization hit her that this was the last time they would ever be together. Her features dissolved into tears. And that was what finally snapped Nick back to his senses. The sight of her shoulders shaking in silent agony was too much for him.

He sat up, pulling her against his chest. "God, I'm sorry. I don't know what got into me. I didn't mean to hurt you."

Her hands snaked around his ribs, squeezing him painfully tight. "Nick, I can't bear it," she sobbed. "What am I going to do without you?"

He stroked her tangled hair. "You'll go on with grace and dignity as you must. With time, you'll get over me and you'll move on with your life. I only hope you remember me fondly when you think back on me."

She burrowed even closer against him.

He whispered into her hair, "Don't forget me, Katy,"

She pulled back far enough to look up at him. "Never!" she declared fiercely. "I won't let anybody forget you!"

They stared at each other for a long time. And then they sealed the promise with a kiss. He kissed her with all the desperation and fury within his soul, and she met his emotions with her own, equally desperate, equally passionate.

The heavily embroidered coverlets landed on the floor in a heap. The satin sheets were cool on Nick's skin as he pulled Katy down to him. Her hair formed a curtain around their faces, and he ran his fingers through its softness before he kissed her again, losing himself in the fathomless blue ocean of her gaze.

Everywhere he touched her she was golden warmth, her skin glowing in the late-afternoon sunlight. She looked like a gilt goddess. He wrapped his arms around her and carried her down to the mattress, worshipping her with his entire body, nearly sobbing with joy in the moment when their flesh and souls became one. Time ceased to exist, and he looked deeply into her eyes, loving her with body and mind.

Mesmerized by the rapture on her features, he stared down at her, memorizing for all time this sight, this moment. When he went to his death, this would be the image he called to mind to carry through the end. His love, his Katy, smiling through the tears of ecstasy and tragedy and love streaming down her face.

His own tears fell, mingling with hers, as they flew together one last time, scaling the untouched heights of pure passion. They soared like eagles, breathless wind racing past, inhaling the freedom of this place they'd made between them.

They paused for an eternity, for an instant of perfection, and then they plunged together, diving earthward with reckless daring, feeling the weightless rush in their stomachs and throats, glorying in the power and beauty of their flight.

But like the eagle, they, too, were bound by gravity and time, and eventually they had to return to earth. Nick became aware of rumpled satin, of Katy lying on his chest, crying quietly. The sun was rapidly sinking out of sight. He had no idea how long Katy'd been with him, but she dared not get caught with him like this or else everything would truly be lost.

It was possibly the hardest thing he'd ever had to do, but he took her by the shoulders and lifted her up gently.

"It's time, my love."

She closed her eyes briefly and then nodded once. He tore his hands off her skin and forced his feet to carry him into the bathroom. He retrieved her clothes and somehow made his hands dress her in them. She stood woodenly, like a mannequin with no pulse, no soul.

He stepped in front of her. She tried to smile up at him, but instead tears spilled out and rolled down her cheeks.

He touched her face and said softly, "I will wait for you until the end of time, my love. Live with joy. Love with passion. And when your days on this earth have ended, come to me. I shall be waiting for you."

She threw her arms around him and sobbed against his chest, "I can't do it, Nick. I can't say goodbye."

He bowed his head and murmured into her hair, "Then merely say as the French do—*au revoir.* Until we meet again."

"I'll love you forever," she cried.

"And I you."

He peeled her arms from around his waist and resolutely turned her to face the door.

"Go now, my darling. And don't look back."

Chapter 10

Katy became vaguely aware of somebody pounding on her hotel room's door. She squinted against the gravel under her eyelids as sunlight streamed in her window. She must have cried herself to sleep at some point last night.

"Katy, it's Larry! Wake up already!"

He sounded urgent.

She dragged herself out of bed and over to the door. She unlocked it and opened it a few inches. "What do you want?" she mumbled, in no mood to deal with anyone or anything right now.

"Get dressed. We've got to go."

"I'm taking the day off."

"Don wants the whole team downstairs in the lobby right now. We've been summoned to the palace. All of us."

"Why?" The cobwebs were slowly clearing from her

mind. The palace was the last place she wanted to be today. Oh, God. *Today.* No. No, no, no! She wasn't going to the palace today of all days.

"Nobody knows. Grab your robes and let's go. The rest of the team's waiting."

"No. I'm not going."

The guy actually threw her a sympathetic look for once. "You don't have any choice. We've been *ordered* to go to the palace. All of us. Now. If you don't go, you'll be arrested."

She groaned. That was probably the one argument that could sway her. She mustn't endanger the potential baby she protected.

Katy hadn't brushed her teeth in twenty-four hours, and her mouth felt furry. She was still wearing the yellow dress from yesterday. "Can I at least go to the bathroom before we leave?" she asked.

Larry shifted impatiently. "Yeah, but hurry."

Sure enough, the whole team was waiting, milling around like a disturbed nest of hornets as she descended the last flight of stairs five minutes later. Before she'd even reached the lobby, Don Ford turned to lead the team to the palace.

Katy stumbled along in the bright sunshine. It was already hot. The sun beat down on her, and the black *abaya* absorbed the heat like asphalt. Before long she felt like an egg slowly frying. They headed up the hill to the palace, but instead of going to the small postern entrance they always used, Don was directed to the main drawbridge.

The enormous courtyard inside was full of rebel

soldiers, and the InterAid team was caught in the crush like a twig tumbling along in a much greater logjam. Katy grabbed the back of Larry's shirt, and somebody grabbed the back of her *abaya* as they struggled to stay together.

The mob's surging movement settled slowly as the crowded square grudgingly accommodated the late arrivals. Then abruptly a great roar went up from around them. Katy looked for the source of their excitement but couldn't see much over the heads of the crowd.

Everybody was looking off to the right. She turned and looked in that direction. And nearly passed out. She sagged, and had the crowd not been so tight, she'd have gone down to the ground.

A gallows stood on a raised platform.

High noon. Death by hanging. Just like one of your cowboy movies.

Oh. My. God.

No. She couldn't stand here and watch Nick die. She couldn't. She just couldn't. She tried to shove her way out, tried to escape the horror. But she couldn't move an inch in any direction. She was trapped.

A small group of soldiers stepped up onto the platform. They parted to reveal a man standing in their midst, shirtless, hands tied behind his back, his head covered with a brown burlap bag.

Her wail was swallowed by the roar of the crowd as the shirtless man was pushed forward. Panic stole any further breath from her. She had to do something! She couldn't stand here and let this happen! But there was nothing to do. Nothing at all. Over a thousand rebel soldiers stood between her and Nick.

In numb horror she watched the noose drop around his neck. Katy felt the rough hemp around her own neck, its fibers scratchy and painful. The hangman tightened it, and her own breathing hitched, constricted by the noose. The knot was adjusted off to the side a bit.

Incongruously, beneath the wild screaming of the crowd, Katy heard Larry's voice beside her saying, "Thank God they put the knot off center."

She leaned close to her partner and shouted in his ear, "Why's that?"

Larry shouted back, his gaze riveted on the platform, "The fall will break his neck this way. He won't suffer. If the knot were centered behind his head, it's possible he wouldn't break his neck and would have to die of suffocation. Can take up to ten minutes."

If it was possible, her horror grew even more.

Her gaze swiveled back to the platform, where some Army general stepped forward, waving a rifle over his head. He made a short speech in Arabic. It amounted to a pep talk whose theme ran along the lines of, "Kill, kill. Blood makes the grass grow!"

Never once did her gaze leave Nick. He stood as still as a statue, never indicating that he heard the accusations being flung against him, never flinching as the general jabbed him a couple times with his rifle for emphasis.

The crowd grew restless and began to shift and sway around her as Sharaf's man whipped them into a frightening frenzy. Under normal circumstances, Katy would be scared witless to be caught in the midst of a violent, volatile mob. But she was too numb, too horrified, too agonized to care. She only prayed that somehow, some way, Nick felt her presence and knew she was with him until the very end.

The crowd shifted, and a couple of tall soldiers in front of her moved apart. For a moment she got an unobstructed view of the platform.

She stared.

Stared some more.

Someone stepped in front of her. Katy shoved the guy aside to stare again.

She ignored the soldier's grumble of complaint as certainty broke over her.

That was *not* Nick standing up there.

She knew every inch of his body. She knew every rib, every bulge of muscle, every nuance of skin over flesh and bone. And that was not Nick Ramsey's chest.

Oh, the build was similar. And this guy had a nice physique. But Nick's stomach was more muscular, his shoulders broader. Overall, this guy was thinner than Nick, with a hint of softness about him that Nick didn't have.

The crowd surged forward as the general's harangue finally drew to a close.

Who was that man under the hood? And where was Nick?

Katy stared in morbid fascination as the noose was tightened one more time and then the hangman stepped to a long lever beside the gallows post.

A mighty roar rose from the crowd, then settled into an ear-splitting chant, repeated until Katy thought she was going to scream. They were calling for the king's death.

The hangman paused, his hand on the lever.

The general gestured and the hangman nodded.

Katy closed her eyes and turned her head away. She could not, would not, stand and watch a man die.

Nick! She screamed silently. *Where are you?*

Filtered light wavered past Nick's eyelids. He became aware that his stomach rumbled with hunger and a touch of nausea. More details registered. He lay on a soft surface, not his customary rock ledge. And wherever he was, it was too bright to be his ten-foot cell. It was an effort against the dragging exhaustion pulling at him, but he pried his eyelids open. He was in a small but elegant bedroom. He frowned. Not the royal bedchamber, either. Glossy wood and silence surrounded him. And something else.

Safety.

He didn't know where he was, but one thing he was sure of: it wasn't Il Leone.

He let his eyes drift closed. He hadn't wasted much time sleeping over the past month on the theory that he had eternity to catch up on his rest. But the exhaustion and stress of living on the edge of death for so long had finally caught up with him. He slipped into unconsciousness once more.

Katy staggered back to the hotel, led by somebody, but she had no idea who. She sat down heavily on the edge of her bed, too in shock to do anything but stare at the walls. *Nick is not dead.*

Thank heavens.

But where was he? The only thing she knew for sure was he hadn't died by hanging at noon. Katy was beside herself with relief that Nick hadn't been the man hanged in the palace. But on another level she was confused. Maybe *even* a little betrayed. He hadn't told her an escape plan was in place. Nor had he contacted her to tell her he was alive. And that worried her. Had Sharaf done something to him worse than hanging? Was Nick alone and in pain somewhere? Or was he safe—already outside of Baraq? At least he wasn't dead.

She hoped.

A droplet of sweat trickled down between her shoulders.

A fly buzzed around her face, trying to land in the corner of her eye. She roused herself to swat it away.

What was she supposed to do with herself now? Her whole reason for being in this godforsaken country was gone. Maybe not dead but definitely gone.

As if in answer to her unspoken question, a knock rattled her door. "Katy?"

It was Hazel Whittaker. She hadn't seen the woman in weeks. Hazel had been assigned to a military base well outside of Akuba and was rarely in the hotel.

Katy dragged her feet across the room and unlocked the door. "Hi, Hazel," she mumbled.

The no-nonsense woman didn't beat around the bush. "Well, as usual, the men don't know what to do with tears. They've sent me in here to deal with you."

"Thanks, but I don't need dealing with. I was just upset by having to watch that poor man be hanged."

"King Nikolas? Yes, that was gruesome. Can't say as I ever had any great desire to see a man die that way."

Katy flinched at the sound of Nick's name. "Look. I'm not going to fling myself out the window or anything. You don't have to hang around patting my hand if you don't want to."

Hazel laughed. "You don't need hand-holding, girl. You're a tough one, you are."

Katy blinked. "Me?"

"Goodness, yes. We all know about the extra work you've been doing with that prisoner-informer you developed."

Guilt speared through her. Her teammates were well-meaning people doing good work for all the prisoners in Baraq. And she'd broken every rule they were all supposed to follow. She'd made a mockery of InterAid's humanitarian mission.

A tiny voice whispered at the back of her brain. *Did Nick make a mockery of me?*

The next time Nick woke up, it was dark and his body ached from lying too long in one position. He was still in the beautifully appointed bedroom. And he still didn't recognize it. *Where am I?*

He threw back the covers and saw he was wearing a pair of silk pajamas he'd never seen before. *Where did these come from?*

He stood and stumbled as the floor shifted beneath his feet. Must've been asleep for longer than he'd realized. He made his way to the crack of light that marked the doorway and reached for the knob to test it. It turned under his hand. *Not locked in, then.* Was this some sort of elaborate mind game his captors were playing? Cautiously he stepped out into the low, narrow hall. And immediately recognized his surroundings. This was a yacht of some kind.

With a hand on the wall to steady himself while he found his sea legs, he made his way down the passageway. It opened out into a stunning salon in shades of white. Lamplight bathed white marble floors, and the walls of windows were black against the night. A low murmur of sound stopped as he stepped into the room.

"Your Highness!"

Kareem. Seated at the far end of the room, with two men whose backs were turned.

Nick stepped forward. "Where am I?"

The other two men faced him. He jolted as he recognized one of them. General George Nagheb. Sharaf's right-hand man. *What the hell?* Had Kareem sold him out? Of all people, Kareem?

The third man—a Caucasian he didn't know—answered his question. "You're on the ship Lucky Strike."

An appropriate name. For surely luck was involved with his being here. The last thing he remembered was finishing his last meal and lying down in his father's bed that last night before his execution.

"And I got here how?"

"A chef at the palace slipped a drug into your supper and—" Kareem paused delicately "—rendered you unconscious. Guards loyal to your family were paid to look the other direction. Your double was sneaked into the palace via the secret passages to your chambers. You were carried out and he was left in your place."

Alarm sliced through Nick. "And what happened to him?"

"He died—God rest his soul in peace—at noon yesterday."

Nick stared. He'd been drugged and sneaked out of the palace? He'd avoided his fate? Again? Yet again he'd failed to act as a king and die at the helm of his nation?

And then the rest of it sank in: another man had died in his place. A bellow of rage built in his gut. He held it back with difficulty.

"You let another man die so that I might live? What were you *thinking?*" His voice rose in fury.

"I—we—were thinking that your nation needs you. That the sacrifice of one man's life was worth Baraq having its rightful king. The man who took your place was a criminal sentenced to death anyway. His family has been taken care of very quietly in return for him agreeing to move up the date of his execution by several months. He seemed pleased to get a chance to make some restitution to society for his crimes before he died."

Nick scowled. That still didn't make it right.

"What's done is done, Your Highness. Accept his gift and move on."

Move on. It wasn't quite that simple. Now the whole world believed him to be dead and—oh, God—Katy. Katy believed he was dead. He lurched in panic. "I have to make a phone call. There's someone I must speak to. I must tell her I am alive."

"Miss McMann?" Kareem asked.

"Mrs. Ramsey," he said through gritted teeth. He searched around the room for a telephone of some kind.

"You will not be able to reach her now. She is on an airplane."

"Bound for where?" Nick asked sharply.

"InterAid was summarily dismissed from Baraq within a few hours of your apparent execution. They were sent to London yesterday, and last I heard, the team is headed back to the United States as we speak."

Nick swore under his breath. He couldn't imagine the suffering Katy must be doing right now, thinking he was dead. "I must get to America right away. Washington, D.C. I have to see her."

Kareem's brow furrowed momentarily, then smoothed out again. Nick couldn't tell if that was consternation or frustration his advisor was doing his best to hide.

Nagheb spoke up. "Forgive me for intruding, but it would not be wise for you to see anyone just now, Your Highness. You must stay out of sight until certain arrangements can be made."

Nick flashed a look of irritation at the general, agitated at the thought of being prevented from seeing Katy right away. "Correct me if I'm wrong, but didn't you support Sharaf in the coup?"

Kareem intervened. "Appearances can be deceiving, Your Highness. Sharaf prepared his coup for months. George and I knew long before your father finally passed away that Sharaf would move the moment your father died. We also knew we did not have the resources or support to stop Sharaf—"

Nick interrupted, "You knew the coup was coming? Why in the bloody hell didn't you tell *me?*"

"Frankly we didn't expect you to stay in Baraq. A grave miscalculation on our part. But in the past you'd made it clear you wanted no part of ruling the country. You must admit, your track record has been…less than committed."

Nick snorted. That was one way of putting it. He gestured for Kareem to go on with his explanation.

The older man pressed on doggedly, "A few of your father's advisors—men that both he and I trusted completely—were approached. Plans were put into place to protect Baraq in the event of a coup d'état. Certain funds were transferred out of the country, and vital documents were removed from your father's office. In a word, we could not prevent Sharaf from seizing power, but we did our best to prevent him from succeeding once he had control of the country."

Nick stared. "I repeat, why in the bloody hell didn't you warn me?"

Nagheb intervened. "I told him not to. If you will forgive my bluntness, you were an unknown quantity. Unpredictable."

"Unpredictable?" Nick laughed shortly. "Let us not mince words, gentlemen—I was completely unreliable."

Nagheb bowed his head briefly in assent. "Also, we did not expect Sharaf to move quite so quickly. But your unexpected decision to stay in Baraq and actually rule, forced his hand. He surprised us all with the speed of his attack."

Kareem took up the narrative. "Thankfully most of our preparations were already complete."

Nagheb chuckled. "You ought to have seen Sharaf's face when he realized the national coffers were completely empty. I must say, he turned a most satisfying shade of purple."

And the pieces started to fall into place. Those large and unexpected deposits in his father's London bank accounts over the last few weeks before he'd died. The couriers arriving with sealed satchels of documents to be put in London safe-deposit boxes. Kareem and Nagheb had been clearing the way for Sharaf to take power and fail while they quietly rescued vital resources from the man.

Nick turned to the third gentleman, who up until now had been sitting quietly, observing the conversation. "And who might you be?"

The pleasant-looking man in his late sixties nodded politely. "My name is John Sutherland. In point of technical fact, I am your stepfather."

"My *what?*" Would the revelations never end?

"Your stepfather. I am married to your mother. And that makes me your stepfather."

"When the hell did *that* happen?"

"Several months ago. I believe you were on a skiing holiday."

"I'm sorry I missed it," Nick said with genuine regret. "Congratulations."

The guy was decent about it and nodded politely. Sutherland added, "Your mother and I arranged portions of your escape from Baraq. This is my yacht, in fact. Your mother took care of the Akuba end of the plan while I set up this end of it."

"My mother went to Akuba? I have a hard time believing that, Mr. Sutherland. When she left twenty-five years ago, she vowed never to go back."

Kareem spoke up. "I believe the concern of a mother for her son overcame her reservations about returning. He speaks the truth. Your mother was instrumental in arranging your escape."

"An escape I did not want, Kareem," Nick growled. "You directly disobeyed my wishes in this matter. I chose to die as the king of my country."

"For what purpose, boy?" Kareem snapped. "What end would your dying serve? The people of Baraq do not have the wherewithal to toss Sharaf and the Army out of power. That must come from foreign powers abroad. Only the legitimate king of Baraq has the clout to secure such assistance. Your people need you. *You* must negotiate for them overseas. *You* must speak for them in the international arena. *You* must procure their freedom from tyranny."

Nick pressed his eyes shut for a moment. "That's all well and good, Kareem. And I may indeed be qualified to do those things. But so are several other able and willing Baraqi citizens of note. You and Nagheb here, to name a couple."

"Do you wish for us to turn this ship around and take you back to Baraq, Your Highness?" Nagheb asked. "If you hand yourself over to Sharaf now, you will look like a colossal fool to the Baraqi people. They would never understand such a sacrifice. They would think the gesture was a waste *and they would be right.*"

Nick began to pace the large salon that suddenly seemed far too small for comfort. Dammit, these do-gooders had tied his hands! Of course, it wasn't as if he actually wanted to die. His overriding sensation at being alive right now was one of profound relief. Now he might get a chance to set Baraq to rights after all, to see his children grow up, to grow old with Katy.

But these guys were missing the point. If he was to go forward as Baraq's king, they had to understand the rules by which he planned to do it—honor and duty being foremost among them.

He spoke slowly, searching for words to explain himself. "I had a great deal of time to think when I was locked in that cell. More time than I cared to have to reflect upon my mistakes in life. And while I was counting my sins, I vowed not to repeat them. I swore to myself and to…someone else…that I would not ever run like a coward again. I promised I would step forth as a king and take what was coming to me. Frankly hanging isn't more than I deserve for the way I've shirked my duty to Baraq over the years."

The three men drew breath to argue, but Nick waved them to silence.

"Yes, I am glad to be alive. But I am deeply disappointed that you did not abide by my wishes. Don't you see what you have done to me? You have made a mockery of what little honor I had left."

Chapter 11

It was good to be home, albeit intensely surreal after the past few weeks. Washington, D.C., her apartment and all the modern conveniences of life were a shock after Akuba, dungeons and martial law. Katy got a little sleep and forced some food down. And waited for a phone call or an e-mail or a letter from Nick. Anything to let her know that her husband was alive.

After three endless days and three even longer nights, her silent, desperate vigil began to take on another dimension. Her period was due any day.

On the fourth day, she couldn't take the guessing game anymore. She went to a drugstore and bought an early-pregnancy test.

Now that the moment was at hand to know whether

or not she and Nick had succeeded in creating an heir to the Ramsey throne, Katy almost didn't want to find out.

Or more to the point, she was afraid of finding out she wasn't pregnant. All of Nick's hopes had rested on this baby. The whole time she'd been in Baraq, she'd wished for it so hard her heart had hurt. What if she wasn't pregnant? All their efforts to save Baraq would have been in vain.

Well, not all in vain. She'd never imagined a love like theirs could exist so quickly or so strongly. She wouldn't give up those precious weeks with Nick even if he had died and she hadn't managed to conceive.

Nonetheless, she chickened out on taking the test. Maybe a bite of lunch first to bolster her courage.

A half hour later she sat in front of the television, eating macaroni and cheese out of the pan, staring at but not seeing a soap opera. She picked at the sticky noodles and their bright yellow-orange sauce congealing into an unappetizing glob.

She was stalling. Hiding like a big dog from what she knew she must do. The test was sitting on her bathroom counter. And the answer wasn't going to change if she waited any longer. Thing was, she didn't feel pregnant. And that scared her to death.

Of course, if she were being honest with herself, she'd admit she was also scared to death over why Nick hadn't called her yet. He knew her cell phone number. He'd asked for it not long after they got married. He'd written it down and put the scrap of paper in his pocket, and he'd had it memorized the next time she'd seen him.

So why hadn't he used it? Was he hurt? Trapped?

Alone somewhere? Had Sharaf and his goons done something dastardly to him in lieu of hanging him? It was hard not to let her imagination run completely amok at the maddening silence from him.

She had to believe Nick had gotten away somehow. Sharaf had desperately wanted him dead. The general wouldn't have substituted another man to die in Nick's place. Someone loyal to Nick must have engineered an escape.

Had it failed? Had Nick died in the escape attempt or maybe later trying to make his way out of Baraq to safety? She could *scream,* she was so frustrated at the total lack of answers!

But there was one answer she could get, darn it.

She stood up and marched into the bathroom. Her insides quailed, but resolutely she pulled out the instructions for the test and followed them. And then she carried the white plastic stick into the living room and sat down to wait. She stared at the little window for the required five minutes.

And then she stared at it some more.

And no matter how much she stared at it, that second blue line wouldn't go away.

She was pregnant.

Nick pressed himself back into the shadows when a pair of men swaggered past as armed and dangerous men tend to do. Escaping the exclusive Washington, D.C. estate his mother and stepfather owned was proving to be more difficult than he'd anticipated.

The guards mustn't spot him! He held his breath. A

few more steps and they'd move beyond his hiding spot. He touched the car keys in his pocket. He could taste freedom. He'd almost escaped.

And then they were past.

He exhaled in relief and darted across the open area between the house and a garage where the estate's utility vehicles were stored. It had been an easy matter to trick the housekeeper by saying that his mother was looking for the keys to the minivan to get something out of its glove compartment. The housekeeper had handed them over without question.

He slipped into the garage and let himself into the vehicle. Sitting on the left side felt exceedingly strange. He'd learned to drive in Britain where they sat on the right side. And in Formula One cars he'd sat in the center. But never on the left.

It wasn't as if he had time to familiarize himself with the car's layout, though. Kareem or somebody would spot his absence sooner or later, and it wouldn't take a rocket scientist to guess where he'd gone.

Nick punched the garage door opener and started the car. When he reached the tall iron security gate at the front of his mother's estate, he punched the handy remote control button for that, too. And then he was free. He pulled out the detailed driving instructions to Katy's house that he'd printed off the Internet, checked the odometer and turned right, as the directions said.

Everyone else was wrong. He knew exactly what he was doing, and it was the right thing to do. Kareem and George's knickers were going to be in a serious knot over this little outing of his, but they could just get over it.

It took Nick about a half hour to make his way across the north side of D.C. And then he was standing at an apartment door, staring at the correct number. He knocked.

Nothing.

He knocked harder. Still nothing.

She *had* to be there. After this escape, his guards would never let him give them the slip again! He pounded some more. In fact, he pounded on Katy's door until a neighbor opened his door and poked his head out.

"She's not there," the elderly man announced.

"Do you know where she is?" Nick asked. "It's urgent that I speak with her right away."

"You might try Rock Creek Park. She likes to walk there. And she went out a little while ago wearing a sweat suit."

The helpful—or more likely just nosy—neighbor gave him directions for how to get to this park. Nick said a quick thanks and headed over.

Katy noticed a man in the distance who didn't belong in the park. It was his coat. Joggers in sweat suits, women with strollers, men in slacks, sweaters and jackets belonged on the lush green walking paths of Rock Creek Park. But a tailored wool dress coat with a suit and tie peeking out from its collar emphatically did not. And then she noticed something else about the man. He was walking quickly. With purpose. Toward her.

There was something about the way he was coming at her, arrow-straight, that made her tense. Or maybe it was the sudden chilling realization that the child inside her already had enemies that would try to kill him or her.

She looked more closely at the man as he approached. From a distance, he looked a bit like Nick. But then, every tall man with dark hair made her think that right now.

The man came closer. He really did look like Nick. Or at least he looked the way Nick would if he was shaved, his nose healed and the bruises faded from around his eyes. He could be Nick's cousin or even brother. He had the same aura of command about him that Nick had, except more of it. A lot more.

She looked away hastily. And started when the man purposely stepped into her line of vision.

"Katy?"

And then she knew. Oh, God. It was his voice. *Nick.*

Elated, she flung herself into him and they staggered as they embraced. His arms nearly crushed her, but she so didn't care. She was probably crushing him, too. She cycled through tears to laughter to indignation that he hadn't contacted her sooner and back to tears. And through it all only one thought consumed her: *Nick's alive!*

Finally, when the shock and relief of his unexpected appearance had worn off enough for her to breathe, he leaned back to smile down at her. "How are you?"

And then she remembered. How was she, indeed! She pulled the white plastic stick out of her pocket and thrust it at him.

He took it, staring down at it in noncomprehension. "What is this?"

"It's a pregnancy test. We did it. I'm pregnant!"

And the wordless, incoherent blend of hugs and tears and laughter started all over again. They both tried to talk at once, laughed again. And finally Nick led her over to a park bench. They sat down, holding hands.

"How did you find me?" Katy asked.

"Your nosy neighbor told me you might be here."

Katy laughed. "God bless Mr. Kramer." Then she said, "Tell me everything. How did you get out?"

"I don't really know. Some of my supporters drugged me, and I woke up nearly two days later on a yacht in the Mediterranean. I'm so sorry I couldn't contact you sooner. I'm involved in delicate negotiations to convince your government and the United Nations to pressure Sharaf into stepping down and handing Baraq back over to me. My advisors felt it would be best to complete the deal in secrecy before the world knows I'm alive. They've had me all but under house arrest."

"How are you here now, then? Is your deal complete?"

"No, no. The deal's far from done. We're still trying to convince the powers that be that I'll be a better political bet than Sharaf. As for how I got here today—I made a run for it. I couldn't wait any longer to see you."

Katy squeezed his hands in silent gratitude. He was so gorgeous. It was hard to imagine they were married and she was expecting their baby. That Baraqi prison cell with its desperation and fear seemed so far away all of a sudden. Another place and time entirely.

"Tell me about the baby."

She smiled. "There's not much to tell. I took a pregnancy test about an hour ago and it came up positive."

Nick's eyes lit with fierce satisfaction. "Thank God I've finally got an heir. That makes my position even stronger in insisting that foreign powers help me regain my throne." He pulled out his cell phone. "I've got to let Kareem know right away. He and George are talking to several government officials right now."

An odd sense of unreality struck Katy. She was sitting on her favorite park bench talking to a *king* about *their* baby! Plain old, everyday Katy McMann. Grace Kelly might land a foreign prince, but not her. And yet, the handsome, poised, intimidating man beside her was all too real. Faint unease rumbled in her stomach.

Katy put a hand out and prevented him from dialing. "Sharaf's supporters will want to eliminate this baby the same way they want to eliminate you. I think it's best we keep this child our secret for now, don't you?"

Nick frowned. "No, I don't. It'll be an important bargaining chip for me to convince your government to help me."

"But I'm barely two weeks pregnant. A lot can go wrong in the early stages of a pregnancy. Let's get through the first trimester before we say anything."

Nick shook his head. "I can't wait that long. I must strike while the iron is hot. The media images of soldiers dying in Baraq are still fresh in the minds of Americans. I can get the backing I need now. Two months from now, some other crisis will have captured your government's attention and I'll be old news. They'll leave me to fend for myself against Sharaf."

Katy frowned as her unease grew into outright alarm. "Nick, I'm not comfortable with this child being used as a bargaining chip. His or her safety has to come first."

Nick's eyes went dark. Guarded. "You're right, of course," he said smoothly.

"I'm serious, Nick."

He nodded. "I understand your concerns. I agree that Sharaf's men are, indeed, capable of trying to harm you and the baby. You must come back to my mother and stepfather's estate and stay with me. There are armed guards, and every security precaution has been taken."

Katy frowned. "If the security's that good, how did you get past it?"

Nick scowled. "I snuck *out.* The security's designed to stop people from sneaking *in.*"

"I'm not crazy about the idea of living surrounded by bodyguards, Nick."

"Then you shouldn't have married a king," he retorted a bit sharply.

"I didn't marry a king," she snapped. "I married a prisoner. A condemned man about to die."

"Do you wish I had died, then?"

"Good grief, no. I'm just saying I don't like the idea of living like a prisoner in my own home. My brothers get death threats now and then, and I've seen how they have to live when they've been threatened. And I don't like it."

Nick shrugged. "There's nothing I can do about that. You married me and slept with me knowing full well you might get pregnant and that you could end up carrying a child Sharaf's people would want to kill."

He was right. But she couldn't very well admit that the thought had never really crossed her mind that carrying this baby would be so dangerous. She'd been so blown away by the idea of making love with Nick that she hadn't really absorbed the other implications of her decision.

But she bloody well saw those implications now.

"Answer me this—once Sharaf is removed from power and you're restored to your throne, will the threat to me and this baby go away?"

Nick didn't even have to stop to consider his answer. "Of course not. There are always crazies out there."

"In other words, I should expect myself and my child to live surrounded by bodyguards and death threats for years to come."

"Yes. I'd say that's a realistic expectation."

Wonderful. Just great. "That's not a particularly pleasant way for a child to grow up." She added dryly, "Not to mention an unpleasant way for me to live."

"I survived it." He shrugged. "There is an upside to being royal. You get to live in a palace and take great vacations. You should see the toys I got for my birthdays."

She wasn't about to let him make light of this situation. She said firmly, "Wealth is no substitute for being safe and loved."

"This child will be safe. That's what bodyguards are for. And this child will certainly be loved," Nick retorted with a certain undertone of indignation. "I know what it felt like when my father ignored me. I would never ignore my own child."

"No, you'd just use a baby as a pawn in your political maneuvering."

"Katy. This child exists. That's a fact. Yes, I'll use any fact at my disposal to help make the case for getting my kingdom back. What's so wrong with that?"

"That *fact* is a baby. A helpless, vulnerable, endangered baby."

Definite exasperation vibrated in his voice now. "I'm

offering you and the baby the full protection of my security team."

"In the first place, it's a lousy way to live. And in the second place, I'm not all that impressed with your bodyguards, given that you're sitting here right now."

"What do you want to do?" Nick's voice began to rise. "Hope this child will just go away? Deny its parentage? Pretend we never got married?"

She glanced up, alarmed, as a pedestrian hurried past, his shoulders hunched in his jacket, the collar pulled up around his ears. Was this her future? Jumping at every stranger who crossed her path?

She turned her attention back to the angry man beside her. He was formidable in his wrath. Definitely king material. Before she'd gone to Baraq she might have wilted under such an onslaught. But now she was a different person. She'd taken chances and faced danger. She'd tested her moral spine and knew its strength. No matter how mad Nick was, she wasn't about to crumble now, not when her child's future rode on it.

"Don't patronize me, Nick. All I'm asking is that you not say anything to anyone about the existence of this child for a while. Let the political situation simmer down. Boot out Sharaf, get your throne back and let the hotheads who followed him get used to the idea of you as king. There will be plenty of time later to announce that you have an heir."

"That's a wonderful plan. But yet again I find myself in a situation where I have no time. I have a few days, maybe a week, to convince your government to help me. Without the backing of the United States, I can forget winning over the United Nations. And without the backing of both, I cannot take back Baraq."

"The way I heard it in Akuba, most people thought Sharaf's government would eventually collapse from the weight of its own greed and infighting."

"Maybe. Maybe not. Even if the Sharaf regime does collapse, who'll step in to take over after him? If I don't make a strong run at the throne now, other players will step onto the field and make a grab at power. The only way to prevent long-term chaos is for me to put an end to anybody else's ideas of snatching Baraq for themselves."

No doubt about it, Nick's logic was sound. But where did that leave Katy and this baby? The answer was bitter on her tongue. It left them playing second fiddle to Nick's obsession with regaining the Ramsey throne.

What in heaven's name was she supposed to do now?

Just as he bent to the floor, Sharaf caught a glimpse of an aide rushing toward him. Irritated, he ignored the aide, who should've known not to disturb him at his prayers. Particularly now, when everything was coming apart at the seams.

He could use all the divine intervention he could get. Baraq's coffers were empty. His top officers were fighting amongst themselves. A few of them were even threatening to defect back to the royalist camp if he didn't cough up the monetary rewards from Baraq's treasury that he'd promised them before he'd found out it was bankrupt.

Finally he climbed to his feet, glaring at the aide who stood there trembling, cell phone in hand.

"A call for you, General. From Major Moubayed."

Moubayed? About damned time. Sharaf snatched the phone and slammed it to his ear. "Tell me some good news," he growled.

"I have located King Nikolas. As you predicted, he was holed up at his mother's home. He finally showed himself this afternoon."

Sharaf's heart leaped. "Excellent!"

"There is more, sir."

"Tell me."

"He left alone and went to visit a woman. They embraced with great passion when they met. He clearly cares for this woman."

Sharaf's mental wheels started to turn. Maybe he could kidnap the woman. Use her to blackmail Nikolas into formally abdicating. Problem: the selfish dog never attached himself to any female seriously or for long.

"She will come and go from Nikolas's life. She is no help to us."

"I overheard King Nikolas ask her if she wished to pretend they'd never gotten married."

Sharaf about dropped the cell phone. "*Married?* When? Who?"

"It is the girl from the InterAid team. The one who visited him all the time in his prison cell in Baraq before we knew he was the king. They must have met then. Maybe they've married in the past few days."

Sharaf's eyes narrowed. Marriage meant sex, and sex meant babies. Or more to the point, heirs. And heirs meant hope for the return of the Ramsey regime to the people of Baraq. Oh, no. That would not do at all. He snapped, "Kidnap the girl. And soon. Before he gets her with child."

He hung up the phone without bothering to wait for Moubayed's reply. The man was no dummy. He knew what rode on stopping Nikolas from reproducing. Everything.

Chapter 12

Katy tossed and turned most of the night, replaying the argument in her head. She saw Nick's point, but he needed to see hers, too. It was all well and good to try to get his throne back, but what good would it do to have the stupid thing if his child weren't alive to inherit it?

The next morning, she dragged herself out of bed and into the bathroom of her apartment, where she duly emptied the scant contents of her stomach. What a time for morning sickness to strike. She managed to sip some chamomile tea and nibble a few crackers and was just starting to feel human again when her cell phone rang.

She was half tempted to ignore it. What was the point of arguing more with Nick? Neither of them was going to change their mind on this one. They both had too much riding on it—he his throne, and she the safety of her baby.

Reluctantly she answered. “Hello?”

“Hi, Katy. It’s Don Ford. Could you come down to the InterAid offices sometime today?”

What in the world? She still had another two weeks of r & r after the Baraq assignment. Why was Ford calling her during her time off? She replied, “Uh, sure. When?”

“As soon as it’s convenient for you. I’ll be here all day.”

She looked at her watch. It was nearly nine o’clock. The worst of the morning rush hour would be over soon. Maybe a little dry toast and some more herbal tea, and then the Metro ride to the InterAid building downtown. “How about ten o’clock?”

“I’ll see you in an hour.”

She frowned at the phone as she hung it up. While he’d been cordial enough, Don had sounded noticeably more formal than usual. What was up with that?

Dread settled heavily in her stomach. Something bad was going down.

Don was not alone when she stepped into his office. Larry Grayson was there, along with several other men Katy didn’t recognize. Don introduced them. They were all on the InterAid board of directors. Their names went past Katy in a blur. What did register was the way they all were frowning at her. Even Larry’s mouth was a tighter white line than usual.

She sat at the conference table with the group and looked at her boss expectantly.

He didn’t waste any time getting to the point. “InterAid has received a complaint from the interim government of Baraq regarding your actions while you were in that country acting as InterAid's representative."

Oh, God.

Ford continued, "General Sharaf has faxed us a report detailing your activities for the three weeks you were in Baraq. And, I have to say, it's most alarming. It alleges that you became personally involved with one of the prisoners, that you bribed guards, that you interacted covertly with women in the city of Akuba and assisted them with illegal activities and that you violated the Geneva Conventions by withholding the identity of certain prisoners."

Wow. Give the general an A-plus for doing his homework! He hadn't missed a trick. Panic hovered just beneath her skin. She didn't want to guess how that information had been obtained. Had young Riki, the guard she'd bribed with honey cakes, been beaten or tortured? Were the women she'd met in Akuba all right? Concern for her acquaintances in Baraq rose up to choke her.

One of the other men at the table leaned forward. "How do you respond to these accusations?"

She didn't have three brothers and a father who were trial lawyers for nothing. She knew better than to blurt out a confession of guilt like a child caught with her hand in the cookie jar. And if she'd learned nothing else from Nick, she'd learned things were never as they seemed on the surface when it came to Baraq.

What was Sharaf up to? Why had he come after her like this? Had he figured out the man his men had hanged wasn't Nick? This complaint smacked of a fishing expedition to draw out Nick.

Katy also knew from her family how to buy time by answering a question with a question. "When did Sharaf file this complaint? And what supporting evidence did he provide? How did he gather this supposed evidence?"

The men acted startled. What? They didn't think a McMann would know how to handle herself under legal pressure? *Surprise, boys.*

Ford fielded her questions. "Uh, the report came early this morning, and he didn't give us any information about how he found all this out. He just listed the activities he was protesting."

And now for a bit of the old best-defense-being-a-good-offense tactic. "What are his demands?" Katy asked. "For surely he wasn't making this little report out of the goodness of his heart. The guy's a war criminal who overthrew a legitimate and peaceful government by force, for crying out loud."

One of the directors cleared his throat. "He's asked for compensation from InterAid in lieu of suing us for malpractice and negligence."

She snorted. "And you're actually thinking about caving in to such a transparent tactic? Tell the guy to go suck an egg. Threaten to summon an international tribunal and put him on trial for war crimes. Starting with him hanging the rightful king of Baraq without a trial."

The men waxed thoughtful at that suggestion.

She leaned back in her chair and crossed her hands over her stomach. She said wryly, "I happen to know a team of attorneys who'd be happy to rake this guy over the coals for you."

While they chewed on that reminder of who her

family was, she gathered her purse and stood. "If you gentlemen would like me to have the McMann Law Firm send him a snappy letter suggesting he cease and desist with these ridiculous threats or if you decide to go ahead and charge Sharaf with war crimes, let me know. I can get you a nice break on the regular hourly rate for the McMann brothers' services. Although God help Sharaf if he actually drags my brothers into court. They'll eat him alive."

And on that not the least bit subtle hint that the McMann brothers could just as easily eat InterAid alive on her behalf, too, she sailed out of the office.

A few minutes later, she sagged in her plastic subway seat, a great deal more nauseous than her pregnancy could account for. How in the world had Sharaf found all that out about her? And why had he bothered? As far as he should know, she was just some anonymous relief worker who'd come and gone. There was no reason he should have singled her out like this.

Did Sharaf know about her and Nick? How could he? *After this morning's business, how could he not?*

Who else knew about her and Nick? How much danger were she and the baby in? One thing was for sure: this latest stunt by Sharaf made her more certain than ever that she and Nick *must not* reveal to anyone the existence of the baby.

She had a bad feeling about this. A really, really bad one. How Sharaf had figured out something was up between her and Nick, she had no idea. At best, he was experimenting to see what happened when he poked at Katy. At worst, he had some truly sinister plan for her.

All of a sudden the Metro felt entirely too claustrophobic. She got off at the next stop and went up into the city to walk around a bit while her stomach settled down.

And then another logical conclusion struck her: Sharaf had to know Nick was alive. Why else would he be investigating and harassing people connected to Nick? She stopped on the street corner, pulled out her cell phone and dialed the phone number Nick had given her yesterday.

Nick answered it personally. "Go ahead," he said curtly.

"Nick, it's me."

Nick's tone shifted drastically to one of warm affection. "Katy. How are you feeling?"

"I'm fine. But we've got a problem."

"Is everything all right?" he asked in quick concern.

"The baby and I are fine—if you call my first bout of morning sickness fine. But InterAid just got a detailed report from Sharaf complaining about my relationship with you in Baraq. He'd have no reason to be poking around over me unless he knew you were alive."

"Damn. I knew he'd find out eventually, but I was hoping it would take longer. I'm running out of time to convince your government to help me." A pause. "I'm sorry, but I've got no choice. I have to tell the State Department about an heir to the throne being on the way. You and our child are American. That will carry a huge amount of weight with your government."

"Nick! Sharaf can't be certain whether or not I'm truly important to you, yet he's already trying to use me against you. Just imagine what he'll try to do to me if he finds out there's a baby! You can't possibly tell anyone about this!"

"Katy, I have no other options. The negotiations are stalled, and unless I bring some new and compelling reason to the table for your government to intervene, it's not going to happen. I'll lose my throne."

"There's got to be some other way. Work through private lobbying groups. Goodness knows, women's-rights groups would be willing to help you, given what Sharaf's doing to women in Baraq."

"I'm sure they would. And getting my throne back that way could take years. Decades. Maybe never."

"What's more important, Nick? Your throne or your child?"

He huffed in what sounded like exasperation. "They're inseparable in my mind. They're the two halves of my Ramsey legacy. I need both to fulfill my duty to my family and my country."

"Dammit, Nick! *We* are your family! Not some palace full of dusty swords on the wall or a cemetery full of dead people. Us!"

"Katy, Ramseys have sat on the throne of Il Leone for a thousand years. I will not be the one to break that chain. I *will* have my throne back and I—and my children—*will* sit upon it again."

Stubborn, pigheaded man! What was it going to take to get through to him? A beep sounded on the phone line.

"That's my call-waiting, Katy, and I need to answer it. Kareem and George are at the State Department again, trying to convince the people over there to work with us."

She hung up, put the cell phone back in her purse and stuck her arm out to hail a cab. Nick was being such a jerk! All he was concerned about was his precious throne. Duty and honor over all.

It wasn't a bad sentiment, just infuriating! No matter that he'd completely imploded her life. No matter that she had no idea how she was going to raise this child with even a semblance of normalcy once word of its existence became public. In this country, it was expensive to buy privacy.

Maybe because she was distracted by that whole new set of worries, she didn't notice the man who walked up behind her. All she knew was that suddenly a man in a black leather bomber jacket had her by the elbow and was crowding her forcibly toward a delivery van that had just pulled to the curb.

It all happened so fast that she barely had time to think about it. The guy who had her arm was strong and quick. She caught a flash of dark hair, a big sliding door opening in front of her and blackness yawning inside.

Maybe it was because she was so furious already that she completely went berserk. Or maybe it was some heretofore dormant mother-protecting-child reaction breaking loose in her. But either way, only one thought exploded across her brain: *nobody* was harming her baby!

She kicked and screamed and scratched. She dropped to the ground when the guy tried to get his arms around her and she rolled against his shins, knocking him off balance, screaming all the while. She glimpsed several passersby stopping. They looked willing to help but unsure what to do.

"Call the police!" she shouted.

One of the bystanders stepped forward and grabbed

her assailant's arm. Several other people stepped forward after the first man took the lead. And her attacker abruptly seemed to think better of taking on an entire crowd. He leaped into the doorway of the van, crouching on its metal floor as it peeled away from the curb.

She looked up in horror just before it left and glimpsed a face she'd hoped never to see again in her life. *Major Moubayed.*

He mouthed down at her, *I'll be back.*

As the van pulled away, she wasn't surprised to see its license plate entirely obscured by mud. Handy, that.

The same man who'd confronted her attacker helped her to her feet. He was a gray-haired businessman in a wool coat and he carried a briefcase. "Are you all right?"

She smiled gratefully at him. "Yes, thanks to you."

He shrugged off her appreciation. "You need to call the police right away, miss, and report that mugger."

The man helped her dust herself off as she replied, "You're right. I will."

Indeed, when a cab finally stopped for her, she asked the driver to take her to the nearest police station. Shaking and fear set in about halfway there. How had Moubayed found her? He couldn't possibly know where she was...unless he'd followed her from the InterAid offices. Of course! Sharaf had to know the powers that be at InterAid would call her immediately about his report. Moubayed knew exactly where she'd be, if not this morning, sometime very soon. All he'd had to do was stake out InterAid headquarters and wait for her to show up.

By the time the cab pulled up in front of the police

precinct, Katy was breathing a little more normally and her knees felt as if they'd hold her weight without buckling. But she still felt shaky all over.

The police were sympathetic and helpful, taking a detailed report and promising to look into whether or not Moubayed was, in fact, in the United States. She didn't believe for a minute, though, that they'd be able to do a darned thing to him if they found him. Even if the police did catch up with him, she'd bet he had a diplomatic passport in his pocket.

Regardless of what the police might find, she *knew* he was out there. Furthermore, he was clearly under orders to snatch her. She emphatically did not want to discover what Sharaf had planned for her when and if Moubayed nabbed her.

This was exactly what she'd feared. She and the baby were in no-kidding danger. She ought to call Nick and tell him about her little encounter with Moubayed, but he'd just insist she come to wherever he was staying and hide behind fences and armed guards. While that might be a reasonable short-term solution, it was not how she planned to live her entire life.

Problem was, it looked as though their secret was already out. Or at least suspected by Sharaf. It didn't take any great thought to figure out why Nikolas Ramsey had married a relief worker he'd just met right before he was likely to die. It probably didn't matter to Sharaf and company whether she was already pregnant or not. She represented the *possibility* of an heir by the simple fact that she was married to Nick.

The whole idea of being Mrs. Nikolas Ramsey still

seemed too strange to be true. Had the beautiful passion between them been real at all? Or had it all been some sort of hallucination fueled by the stress of the whole situation?

Who was Nick Ramsey really? She barely knew him at all. And the man she was dealing with now bore little resemblance in any way to Prisoner 1806.

Reluctantly she dialed Nick's phone number. He didn't answer. She figured he must be on the other line discussing a matter of state with his advisors, again. She left him a message describing the attack and naming her attacker and then told him she was heading to her parents' house.

She was being forced into hiding, darn it. But at least it would be on her terms and not Nick's. Nonetheless, she didn't like having to hide one bit. There had to be *something* they could do to get rid of Sharaf.

It was probably time to fess up to her family anyway. Her brothers and father were four of the smartest human beings she'd ever met. And frankly her mother was right up there with them. If anyone could cook up a plan to restore Nick's throne and remove Sharaf not only from power but from Katy's and Nick's lives, it would be the collective McMann clan.

Besides, what else was family for if not rallying in a crisis?

Chapter 13

Nick stepped into the walnut-and-leather inner sanctum of the McMann Law Firm, Katy's oldest brother Travis's office. Katy's brother looked a lot like her but with hazel eyes and light-brown hair. The same great bones, though. Classic good looks. Women jurors must swoon over him. "Mr. McMann, my name is Nikolas Ramsey."

The attorney looked up in surprise. "As in the King of Baraq?"

"That's correct."

Travis stood and came around his desk. "Is it proper to shake hands with you, Your Highness?"

Nick laughed. "I don't know. My advisors are still training me in such things." He stuck out his own hand and the two of them duly shook.

"Have a seat. Can I get you some coffee?"

"No, thanks. Your secretary already got me some."

McMann went behind his desk and sat. "I have to say, I'm surprised to see you. I was under the impression you—" a delicate pause "—were no longer with us."

Nick laughed. "How did Mark Twain put it? Rumors of my demise have been greatly exaggerated?"

"Apparently. What can I do for you today?"

"I need your help. I need to depose a dictator and I think you're just the man to help me do it."

Travis looked startled for a moment, which in a trial lawyer of his caliber meant he must be mightily surprised.

"Why me?"

"Because you're family."

"I beg your pardon?" Travis showed surprise for a second time, but it was more quickly masked.

"Perhaps I had better start at the beginning."

"Good idea." Travis leaned back in his chair and steepled his fingers just as Nick's lawyer in London did when he went into listening mode.

Instead of talking, Nick dug out his wallet. He pulled out a one-dollar bill, laid it on the desk and pushed it across the green leather blotter toward Travis.

"What this?" Katy's brother asked cautiously.

"A retainer fee. I'd like to hire you as my lawyer. I don't have a lot of cash on me at the moment, but I've got about five billion in my bank account, if you accept checks."

"This works just fine," McMann said with a chuckle as he took the dollar bill and deposited it in a desk drawer. He added dryly, "I gather, then, I don't need to go over my hourly fees with you before we begin this conversation."

Nick replied equally as dryly, "No, you don't."

"So. From the beginning, then," Travis prompted.

Nick told him everything from the moment he got the phone call from Kareem telling him his father had died. He told of coming home, the funeral, the miserable state of the government, his plans for Baraq. Then the coup and hiding in jail as a common soldier. He took a deep breath and continued on, describing meeting Katy and conceiving a plan to leave behind an heir before he died.

Travis's jaw rippled at that part. But then, he was Katy's big brother. He was authorized to be outraged on her behalf. Nick pressed on into how she'd agreed to marry him and how he'd arranged their wedding.

Travis interrupted him at that point, exclaiming, "Are you telling me you're *married* to my sister?"

Good thing Nick had put Travis on retainer before he'd told this tale. Otherwise, he got the distinct impression Travis might've leaped across his desk and punched him.

Nick replied, "That's correct. And for the record, I love Katy and intend to stay married to her if she'll have me."

Travis's eyes narrowed and his jaw clenched, but he managed to say, "Continue."

Nick omitted any mention of the mind-blowing love-making that ensued after their wedding and skipped right to the part where George Nagheb walked into his prison cell and asked King Nikolas to go with him. He concluded with a brief summary of how his advisors faked his death and spirited him out of Baraq to Washington, D.C., so he could negotiate for intervention and recover his throne.

Nick finally fell silent. Telling the story dredged up

all the failure and despair of those weeks again. He was left feeling drained even now. It seemed as if he'd imagined it all, as if that whole agonizing month had never happened. It was enticing to just forget, pretend everything was fine, to take his billions and go live a life of leisure on the Riviera. Why put himself at risk again? He'd been incredibly lucky to escape Baraq with his life the first time. Why tempt fate?

And then he pictured the filthy, frightened faces of his fellow prisoners. Men who'd been willing to die for him. He thought of the bereaved families of the men who *had* died for him. He remembered the horror in Katy's voice as she'd described women being flogged in the square.

He envisioned the face of a baby. His baby. He was going to be a *father*—a role model to a son or daughter—and that changed everything.

"How are your negotiations going?" McMann asked.

"They're not. The United Nations refuses to do anything unless the United States first agrees to support me. And the U.S. isn't showing any interest in interfering in the internal politics of another nation."

"You have a plan to break this stalemate, though, or you wouldn't be sitting here. Correct?"

Nick nodded. "That is correct. But before I get to that, I need to tell you about one more complication to this scenario."

"Lay it on me."

"Your sister and I are expecting a baby."

That brought Travis straight out of his chair. "What?"

Retainer fee be damned, this guy was a brother first and foremost and he obviously cared a great deal for his sister. That pleased Nick. Although he could really do without a big-brotherly black eye.

Nick nodded. "I couldn't be more pleased. I'm hoping the baby gets Katy's beautiful blue eyes and her kind heart."

That seemed to mollify Travis a bit. He subsided into his leather chair once more. But Nick fancied he saw a thin stream of steam rising off the top of Travis's head.

Nick gave him a moment to collect himself and then said, "And now for the last bombshell. One of Sharaf's men tried to kidnap Katy earlier this afternoon." When McMann really did look ready to come over the desk this time, he added hastily, "I've spoken with her and she's safe and at your parents' home."

McMann looked as though he could use a stiff drink. Nick waited until the attorney finally nodded for him to continue.

"That brings us to the present moment. Katy believes we should say nothing to anyone about the baby or else we'll endanger the child's life. I happen to disagree. At this point, Sharaf obviously knows Katy and I are married, and her life is in the same amount of danger whether or not he knows she's pregnant."

McMann nodded. "I'd say your logic is sound. So what do you plan to do about it?"

"The most important thing is to secure my family's safety. Secondarily I want my throne back. And I can achieve both if I can get rid of Sharaf."

McMann nodded cautiously. He looked worried that Nick was going to ask him to arrange for a hit man.

"As a short-term measure, I want to give Katy the entire contents of my London bank accounts. If Sharaf wants Baraq's money, which I happen to know he does—desperately—he'll dare not kill her. He may still try to kidnap her, but hopefully his greed will prevent him from letting his assassins murder her outright."

"And your throne?"

"I need to arrange a press conference. I want to introduce Katy to the world as my wife. I plan to declare her my queen and announce that we are expecting an heir to the throne. And then I plan to pressure the living hell out of your government to support my country and its American queen and heir."

"Little Katy a queen? Who'd have thunk?" McMann shook his head. And then the lawyer went silent. "And you're sure the United States will back you when they find out about Katy?"

Nick replied, "That's where you come in. I think you would be a better negotiator for me with the State Department than my advisors. We do not know the American mind as you do. Katy thinks you are the best litigator in the entire country. Plus, you're family. You have a vested interest in seeing Katy safe. Who better to argue my case?"

McMann challenged, "Tell me one thing—are you going to be a decent king?"

Nick answered without hesitating. "I'll do my very best. And with Katy at my side, I'm confident we'll do right by Baraq."

McMann replied slowly, "That's a hell of a gauntlet you've just thrown at my feet."

Nick looked McMann squarely in the eye. "Will you pick it up?"

Katy's parents took the news that she'd gotten married and was expecting a baby surprisingly well. She got the impression they were glad at the order the two events had occurred in. Once they got over the initial shock, her mother immediately went into raptures over the arrival of her first grandchild, while her father latched on to the threat to her life.

Despite her protests, he called the security firm her brothers used, and the company sent over a couple men right away to keep an eye on Katy. Thankfully the pair of big, silent men chose to stand watch outside her parents' home rather than hover around her. That would've driven her crazy.

As it was, panic tickled just below the surface of her thoughts, ever present and so close she could reach out and touch it. She really, really didn't want to die.

It took her a while in the familiar surroundings of her parents' house to relax enough to identify the other insidious and even deeper source of her panic.

She was scared to death over her disagreement with Nick. What business did she have being married to him if she couldn't wrap her brain around this obsession of his with his country? It was a noble and entirely understandable quality in a king to be so committed to his people. But she wasn't all that sure it translated into being a good husband and father.

If only she'd had any idea of all the baggage that came with Nick when he'd first asked her to have his baby!

Would she have still said yes?

That was the sixty-four-thousand-dollar question, wasn't it? She sighed. Those glorious stolen moments in his arms seemed a world away and a lifetime ago. If the two of them could somehow recapture that incredible chemistry, there would be no question but that she'd do it all over again.

But doubts kept insinuating themselves into her thoughts. Was he just an incredibly skilled lover who'd pleasured her outrageously while staying emotionally detached himself? Or had that time been as magical for him, too? If only she knew where his heart lay for sure.

The phone rang and Katy's mother glanced at its digital face. "Oh, it's Travis calling from his office. He really should work less. Maybe then he'd find himself a nice girl and give me some grandchildren, too."

Her mother picked up the phone. "Hello, dear." A pause, then gasped, "Oh. My goodness, I'm so sorry. Yes, she's right here."

Katy looked up in surprise.

"It's your young man, Katrina. He'd like to speak with you."

"Nick?"

"That's right, honey." Her mother put her hand over the receiver as she walked the telephone handset to Katy. "And he has a very nice voice."

Katy rolled her eyes and took the phone. "Wait till you see him. He's got a very nice everything."

She put the phone up to her ear. "Hi, Nick."

"Very nice, am I? Glad to hear you think so."

Katy laughed. "You are and you darn well know it. What can I do for you?"

"Aah, it's nice to hear your laughter again. Are you all right?"

"I'm fine." The laughter faded from her voice.

"Do you have guards at the house with you now or should I send mine over?"

"Good grief, no! Keep your own bodyguards. You need them as much as I do. A couple giant thugs in black leather jackets with suspicious bulges under their armpits are outside now."

"Thank God," Nick said in heavy relief.

"So what are you doing calling me from Travis's office?"

"Your brother and I have spent a most productive afternoon together. He's a very bright fellow."

She groaned. "You didn't just say that in front of him, did you? He's insufferable for days after anyone tells him how smart he is."

It was Nick's turn to laugh. "I like your brother a lot. I also hired him to be my attorney. He's helping me implement a strategy to get rid of Sharaf so the three of us can get on with our lives in peace."

Three? It took Katy a heartbeat to figure out who Nick was referring to. And then her heart tripped and stumbled for another beat.

"Darling," Nick continued. "I need you to do me a favor. I'm going to send someone over to pick you up in a little while. I need you to put on some nice clothes—conservative-business-suit sort of clothes—and join me."

"What's going on?"

"I'd rather not say over the phone," he said apologetically.

"Does this have to do with whatever you and Travis cooked up?"

"Indeed it does."

"I don't know whether to be put at ease by that or scared silly."

"Well, what we're planning affects your future, too. It seemed right to involve you in it, as well."

"That does it. I'm scared silly."

He laughed lightly. "Just put on a suit and I'll have someone come over and get you."

"Okay."

"And Katy?"

"Yes?"

"I love you."

She melted on the spot. Who cared if he was a king and she had to share him with an entire nation? How could she not love this man?

"I love you, too."

Her parents were both watching her intently when she hung up the phone. Heat climbed her cheeks. To distract them, she said, "Nick has hired Travis, and the two of them have some plan they want to run past me. Mom, could I borrow a suit from you?"

"Of course, honey."

The two of them went upstairs to find something for Katy to wear. Since she'd lost weight in Baraq, she was much more similar to her mother in build. They picked out a royal-blue cashmere suit that magnified the color of Katy's eyes until they glowed cobalt. The asymmetric cut of the jacket was timeless yet stylish. The suit wouldn't pass for casual anywhere, but it could pass for varying degrees of formal. Since she had no idea what Nick and Travis were up to, she wanted to cover all her bases.

Katy's mother put her hair into a French twist for her, and Katy borrowed some of her mother's makeup. The end effect was startling. It was the first time Katy had really gussied herself up since she'd come back from Baraq, and she didn't clean up half bad nowadays. It must be the good bones Nick had once told her she had.

But then the ever-present doubts began to creep back in. Did he *really* love her? He was surely polished enough and smart enough to manipulate her emotions. Was he saying what she wanted to hear because she was carrying his baby or because he really felt that way about her?

If only they could've fallen in love under normal circumstances. *Yeah, right.* As if she'd have ever crossed his path, let alone caught his eye.

She became aware of a noise outside. It was loud and getting louder. And then her father called from downstairs, "Katy, there's a helicopter about to land in the backyard. I think it's for you."

Thank goodness her parents had a large treeless space behind their house. She called down the stairs, "Either it's for me or you've hooked up with a really rich mistress on the side. Better watch out. Mom'll kill you if she finds out!"

Her mother laughed and walked her down the stairs. Her father looked up when she walked into the family room and stared. "Honey, you look beautiful."

There went the blush again. "Thanks, Dad. I don't know when I'll be home. Don't wait up for me."

He grinned. "Do try to keep the noise down when you come in."

They were having to yell over the din of the helicopter, which was idling in the backyard.

One of the security guards poked his head in the door and shouted, "One of you call for a chopper ride?"

"That would be me," Katy shouted back.

Both guards fell in beside her as she walked across the yard toward the helicopter. How cool was this? A helicopter to pick her up? There were going to be some definite perks to this whole royalty business.

A spotlight turned toward her from the vicinity of the aircraft's cockpit. It reminded her of the lights mounted on police cars. Squinting into the glare, she had no trouble picking her way across the lawn. But she couldn't make out anything other than a big, black blob where her ride awaited.

A door swung open and a man leaned out. One of her security guards stepped forward, and the man from the helicopter said, "We won't be needing you. There aren't any extra seats. We'll take it from here."

The security guard nodded and stepped back. He helped the guy from inside fold down a set of steps and then he helped Katy climb them. After the piercing light outside, she was completely blind in here. She made out the silhouettes of men filling the other three seats in the back, but beyond that all she could see were bright spots dancing before her eyes.

The door shut behind her and the helicopter lifted off. It lifted straight up, and her parent's house fell away beneath her. Then, it tilted forward thrillingly and accelerated away into the night.

Gradually her vision cleared and she was able to see the men around her. She didn't recognize any of them. They were all dark-haired and olive-complexioned. They looked Baraqi. Nick must have sent his personal bodyguards for her after all.

After about fifteen minutes, she turned around to face the cockpit area and the two men seated there. "Where are we going?" she shouted. She'd assumed this would be a short hop downtown to Travis's offices or maybe to a restaurant for a meeting.

The man in the copilot seat turned around to face her.

"Welcome aboard, Miss McMann. Or should I say, Mrs. Ramsey?"

Oh. My. God.

Major Moubayed.

Chapter 14

Nick closed his eyes while a makeup artist put powder on his forehead to eliminate any glare from the camera lights. He hated wearing makeup but was no stranger to it. Between photo shoots for magazines, official portraits and the rare press conference over the years, he was used to paper towels stuck down his collar and fussy makeup artists fluttering around him.

"Ten minutes, Your Highness," a State Department aide told him.

"Thank you. Is my wife here yet?"

"Not yet, sir. We've got a call in to the driver to give us an estimated time of arrival."

She should've arrived fifteen minutes ago. Pressure was building behind his eyes, and his gut was roiling in a way that had nothing to do with stage fright. Something was wrong. He could feel it.

He pulled the paper towels out of his collar and looked at one of his bodyguards. "Bring me my cell phone," he ordered quietly.

Had she stood him up? Had the same sense of unreality that he'd fought ever since he left Baraq overwhelmed her? She'd taken such huge risks in Baraq. Had her courage failed her now? Or maybe being back home made her realize how crazy they'd both been in Baraq.

Dammit! They almost had it all. She just had to hang in there with him for a few more days. Maybe even a matter of hours!

He dialed her cell phone number. No answer.

Surely she hadn't learned what he and Travis were up to and bolted. He'd intentionally given her no hint as to what tonight's rendezvous was about. He'd talked it over with Travis, and while they felt bad for sneaking up on her like this, they both felt it would be unwise to give her advance warning that she was about to be declared Queen of Baraq and presented to the world. She would likely get worked up over it, and they didn't want to make her nervous or stressed. She was expecting a baby, after all.

Nick huffed in frustration as he was transferred to her voice mail. What in the world was going on? She'd been so cheerful on the phone just an hour ago. What had changed between now and then? Why didn't she want to talk to him?

"Ah, there you are, Your Highness. Are we all set on the order of events?" It was an Undersecretary of State who would be participating in the press conference to announce America's commitment to back Nikolas Ramsey in regaining his throne.

Once the State Department had learned of his pretty, young American wife and the child on the way, Travis had helped them see the public-relations nightmare it would be if they didn't get behind the Cinderella fairy tale and help Katy and Nick regain their thrones. Nick suspected Travis's reputation for blatantly and brilliantly manipulating the press to his own ends was largely responsible for the State Department's quick capitulation. They were terrified of what he'd do to them if they didn't go along.

A high-ranking United Nations official had already called Nick to tell him the U.N. would be getting on board, as well, and would issue a press release in the morning. Everything was falling into place. All he and Katy had to do was get through this press conference and then let international pressure push Sharaf right out of power. And in the meantime, maybe they could get away and take a real honeymoon somewhere.

His mental debate over heading for snowy mountains or a tropical paradise was interrupted by a commotion among the cluster of aides who'd accompanied the Undersecretary of State.

One of them rushed toward him and the Undersecretary.

"There's a problem, gentlemen."

The pressure behind Nick's eyes became stabbing pain, and his entire gut rolled over.

"Mrs. Ramsey has disappeared."

Nick expected an explosion from deep in his gut, but instead terror so cold it froze him from the inside out overtook him. "What has happened?" he bit out.

"When our driver showed up, her parents told him she'd left a few minutes before by helicopter to join you."

"Was there a mix-up of some kind? Did the State Department accidentally send one for her in addition to the car?"

"No, Your Highness. I just got off the phone with our flight coordinators, and no helicopters have been dispatched this evening."

"You're about to dispatch one now," Nick snapped. "Call your air-traffic-control centers and find out where that helicopter's gone. And get me another helicopter. I'm going after my wife!"

"One of our security specialists is already working on getting it tracked."

The Undersecretary piped up. "The press conference is set to begin in less than ten minutes. What are we going to do about that?"

"I don't give a damn!" Nick exclaimed.

"I can't very well announce that we're going to back your return to the throne of Baraq until you present your wife. Otherwise it would look like we were reversing course without any good reason for it. The press release has already gone out stating that you've given the entire assets of the Baraqi treasury to your wife. You have to follow up with announcing your wedding or the international press will go ballistic by tomorrow morning. We've only got an hour or so before the European morning newspapers go to print."

As if Nick cared about press brouhahas or the State Department's public image—or about his throne, for that matter! And then it hit him. He didn't give a flip whether or not he ever set foot in Baraq again, let alone became king. All that mattered now was Katy and her safety.

He turned to the State Department official "Look. You deal with it. Say whatever you want to the press. Cancel the damned press conference, for all I care."

"But our agreement… Of course we need to postpone the press conference—your wife's safety comes first. But the timing of this announcement is critical—"

Nick walked away from the guy. He grabbed the aide by the elbow and steered him back over to the now-agitated cluster of other aides, most of whom were talking tensely into their cell phones. He overheard enough snippets of conversations to know these guys were calling in everyone and his uncle to search for Katy. He gave them about a minute before his own impatience got the best of him.

"What have you got?" he asked them as a group.

"The helicopter headed northwest out of D.C. at a high rate of speed. It went off radar about thirty minutes after it showed up."

"Take me there," he ordered.

One of the lead agents nodded. "Police and FBI agents are heading into that area to begin a search on the ground, and the FBI is scrambling a search-and-rescue team by helicopter. We figured you'd want to be there. We'll have a car here for you in approximately ten minutes."

They were the longest ten minutes of Nick's life. He'd had some rough moments when the coup d'état had taken place in Baraq and he'd been waiting to die, but this was a hundred times worse. A *thousand* times worse. He paced like a caged lion and gave serious consideration to doing some random violence if that car didn't get there pretty soon.

Finally an aide gestured to him and Nick rushed to the guy. They rode an elevator to the ground floor of the building and then jogged to a loading dock at the back.

The FBI vehicle pulled up, a big, black SUV. It turned sharply in the tight confines, and Nick ran toward it with Travis right behind him. A door opened in the back and the two men jumped inside. The door hadn't even shut before the SUV leaped forward. The driver opened his window as they hit the streets and slapped a red-and-blue flasher light on the roof. It attached magnetically with a sharp thud.

Nick put on the headset someone held for him. "What's the latest?" he called over the noise and the rush of wind from the still-open window.

"We have a report of a chopper matching the description of ours landing close to a wooded area in Montgomery County. We should be there in twenty minutes."

I'm coming, Katy. Hang on, my darling.

Katy looked around. The helicopter had set them down near the edge of a large field, and Moubayed's men had hustled her to the edge of a dark wooded area as the helicopter had lifted off into the night again, all its lights extinguished. It looked like little more than a shadow as it winged off.

Fear, panic and *terror* didn't begin to describe the emotions gripping her by the throat and barely allowing her to breathe. It was her worst nightmare—and worse—come horribly true.

She reviewed what she recalled of Moubayed from Baraq. It had infuriated him to have his authority challenged or even questioned, and he'd expected her as a female to bow and scrape at his feet. She tried to think of something submissive to say to him that would open a dialogue with him. Maybe allow her to talk him out of killing her right away. Maybe buy herself time to be discovered missing and rescued.

Nick! Where are you?

The worst had happened. Everything she'd warned him about had come to pass. Sharaf's people had found her. And worse, they knew she'd married Nick. She and the baby were so dead. Had Nick backed off trying to retake the throne, had he taken his wealth and his family and just gone away to live a quiet life, she wouldn't be in this mess now. Why, oh why, hadn't he listened to her?

She was startled out of her desperate thoughts when Moubayed snapped, "Someone wishes to speak with you."

Katy looked around the deserted field in surprise. "Here?"

He pulled a cell phone out of his jacket and dialed a number quickly. He spoke in rapid Arabic, but she caught the gist of the conversation. It ran along the lines of, "Yes, she's here. That's right, unharmed. You made it very clear that at all costs we are not to hurt her."

Hearing that was a giant relief. She wasn't out of danger yet, but the immediate threat of death subsided to a dull roar in the back of her head.

Moubayed continued in Arabic, "No, Nikolas doesn't

know we have her. No, sir, I haven't asked her about the money. I haven't said anything at all to her, just as you instructed me. Yes, sir. Here she is."

The cell phone was abruptly thrust at her and Moubayed snapped, "Speak in French."

"Uh, âllo?" she said hesitantly.

"Is this the McMann girl? The InterAid worker who married Nikolas Ramsey in secret and helped him escape?"

Oh, God. She knew that gravelly, demanding voice. She was speaking to Hamzad Sharaf himself.

"General Sharaf?" she asked incredulously.

"Answer the question, girl!" he snapped.

"Uh, I'm Katy McMann and I work for InterAid, but I don't know anything about the rest of that stuff."

"Don't lie to me. I have a copy of your marriage license on my desk. These are a matter of public record in Baraq."

She had no way of knowing if he was bluffing or not. She didn't respond to his comment. Instead she asked politely, "You wished to speak to me?"

"Yes. Let us get straight to the point. I know about the money."

"What money?"

"Don't play stupid with me. The press release was handed to me over an hour ago."

"What press release? I promise I have no idea what you're talking about."

He answered scornfully, "The press release announcing that all of the assets of the Baraqi royal treasury have been transferred into your control."

If she'd had a mouthful of any fluid at that moment,

she'd have spewed it all over Moubayed's chest in front of her. "I beg your pardon?" she blurted in genuine shock.

"You heard me."

She thought fast. Well, then. That explained why she was still alive and why Moubayed was under orders not to harm her. Sharaf wanted to get his paws on all of Nick's millions! She and the baby might still have a fighting chance of getting out of this mess alive. If she could offer him a deal, maybe to trade some of the money for her freedom....

He was speaking again. "I wish to make a trade with you."

She jolted. Had he read her mind?

"What sort of trade?" she asked cautiously.

"I want Baraq. You want what? Your life? That of your husband, perhaps? A certain amount of security for your future?"

Although panic still hovered close, she pushed it aside. She had to keep her wits about her to keep thinking her way through this mess.

She got the distinct impression Sharaf wasn't talking about financial security here. "I am interested in all of those things, yes." Thank goodness he hadn't said anything about a baby. Maybe the child was still safely a secret after all.

"This is what I have in mind. You give me the money. All of it. And in return, I let both of you live."

She wanted to fall to her knees and sob in relief at the offer, to take it in abject gratitude and run. But she was a McMann, dammit, and she knew better. Sharaf was too canny an old codger to make his best offer right away.

She took a deep breath for courage and said lightly, "If we keep all of Nick's money, the two of us will be able to buy more than enough security to stay alive very nicely, thank you. And then we'll still have the rest of it for ourselves."

"Greedy bitch," Sharaf snarled.

She didn't bother to respond to that. She only said, "You'll have to do better, General."

He sighed theatrically. Grumbled about her being a pushy American. Hemmed and hawed about what he could do to sweeten the deal for her when he had nothing to trade with her except her life. And then he finally coughed up his offer. "You give me the money. You and Ramsey live. Plus, he formally abdicates his throne and names me ruler. In return, I will name your first child heir to the throne. When I die, a Ramsey will get the throne back."

Katy sucked in her breath hard. *Wow.* She hadn't seen that one coming! It was more than she could've possibly hoped for! Exultation shot through her. She and Nick and the baby could be a family after all! Their children could grow up in safety. They could live a normal life without any of the stresses and distractions of royalty. Maybe twenty or thirty years from now, one of their children would eventually rule Baraq....

And Nick would never fulfill his destiny. He would never be king. He would never get a chance to make his vision for Baraq's future real. He would have to set aside all he was and all he dreamed of becoming if she took this deal.

She'd get what she wanted and he'd get nothing of

what he wanted. Her conscience pricked her. Could she do it? Could she rip the heart out of everything that Nick was? Would he be able to live with her after she did that to him? Did she want to live with the man who would be left behind if she destroyed his dreams, his very future?

She stalled for time while her thoughts spun wildly. What to do? "What guarantee do I have that you would honor such a deal, General? You'd get the cash, but I'd have nothing but words to go on."

"I will put it in writing. I'll sign it into law."

Aah, he sounded a little desperate now. He wanted this deal very badly indeed. "I'll give you half the money and you leave Baraq. Nick retakes the throne and our children after him, and you never darken Baraq's doorstep again."

Sharaf snorted. "I already rule Baraq."

She retorted, "I already have all the money. Which means you're broke. How are you going to run a country with no cash? In a few months, when food and fuel start to run short and you've got nothing with which to buy more, the Baraqi people are going to get hungry and cold. And they're going to blame you. How long do you suppose they'll stand for that? You've just demonstrated to them that uprisings are entirely possible."

That earned her a long silence from Sharaf and a low snarl from Moubayed. She ignored the major and concentrated on her foe at the other end of the phone line. She could practically hear Sharaf mulling it over. How her brothers played chicken like this for a living, she had no idea. She felt as if she was going to throw up. *C'mon, Sharaf. Take the deal.*

The he said, "I get all the money, and in twenty years I step down and hand the throne over to your eldest child regardless of my health. Or, if I should die before then, your child immediately inherits the throne."

He talked about this stuff as if it were no more than an elaborate game. *I'll trade you my railroads for Boardwalk and Park Place.* Except real lives hung in the balance.

She closed her eyes in indecision. What would Nick do? But then, that wasn't really the question, was it? What would *she* do?

And then something odd happened. A face popped into her mind. Riki, the young Baraqi guard whom she'd bribed with honey cakes. And then another. Hanah, the hotel operator and closet women's-rights activist who'd risked so much to make contact with her. The shopkeepers she'd bought snacks from. And everywhere she'd gone in Baraq, the haunted, desperate eyes of women appalled and terrified by what was happening to them.

Was she courageous enough to do the right thing? After all, this wasn't just about her. This was about the future of an entire nation.

Suddenly she understood. Now she knew were Nick's passion came from. It wasn't an overdeveloped sense of duty to *country* at all! It was his sense of duty to, of loyalty to, of love for the *people* of Baraq that drove him.

Dammit. Why did she have to have that particular revelation now? It would've been so much easier to make the selfish decision and move on with her life in blissful ignorance.

Did she have what it took to measure up to Nick's standards? If she was going to be his wife—heck, his queen, the Baraqi people's queen!—did she have the moral spine to look death in the face? Nick had done so with dignity and grace. But what about her?

Another revelation broke over her. This was how he'd been able to turn down all her offers of assistance, her pleas to run away from Baraq. Being king was bigger than him.

And being queen was bigger than her.

Sharaf's offer was incredibly tempting. A remembered image of Nick's face crossed her mind's eye. It was the day they'd identified him and moved him to the royal apartments. He'd been standing at a window looking out across the city of Akuba before he'd known she'd entered the room. And his face had shone with love. He loved his country. Loved his people. The same way she loved him and the baby inside her.

Certainty settled in her heart.

She knew what she had to do.

Chapter 15

As their SUV raced northwest out of the city and toward Katy, Travis looked at Nick grimly. "Although it's far from the most important problem we've got right now, you do realize you may have blown the deal with the U.S. State Department by walking out on that press conference and leaving them hanging in the lurch, don't you? Now they have the ammunition to pull out of their deal with you."

Nick nodded impatiently. "If it comes down to a choice of the woman I love and my child over my throne, I'll take Katy and the baby."

He paused, startled. One short hour ago, he wouldn't have been so quick to say that. Funny how everything could change so fast. But then, life could be like that. In one week his father died, he became king and he nearly died in the coup. And now in a single day he had a family to protect and his priorities had totally shifted.

Travis looked at him keenly. "Are you sure you choose family over kingdom?"

"Absolutely."

"You really do love her, don't you?"

"More than life." They were silent for a few moments, then Nick said reflectively, "A few weeks ago I was willing to give up my life to be king of Baraq. And now I'm willing to give up my life and my kingdom in the name of being a husband and father."

Travis smiled. "Life is strange, isn't it?"

"Gentlemen," the driver interrupted them. "Air-traffic-control says a helicopter has just popped up on radar right about where Mrs. Ramsey's bird was last seen going off radar."

"Let's go get her," Nick said grimly. "At all costs, my wife *must not* come to harm."

"Understood, Your Highness. Our people have been briefed on the rules of engagement. Mrs. Ramsey is a nonexpendable resource."

The next few minutes were pure hell for Nick. Their SUV, along with several others full of FBI SWAT team members, drove like bats out of hell toward the unidentified chopper. There were a few hairy moments while the SUVs made adjustments in course on deserted country roads to track their target's flight path. But then the pedals went to the metal again.

The clock was ticking. Nick's nerves stretched thinner and thinner. *Hang on, Katy. Don't give up.* He prayed hard that the same unquenchable optimism that had gotten her through the coup would see her through this crisis.

He listened tensely on the radio as the FBI chopper apparently did some nifty flying and eventually forced the target helicopter to land. The SUV arrived on the scene a few minutes later.

Nick waited in an agony of impatience as he was told to stay put and let the SWAT team swarm Katy's helicopter. And then one of the FBI agents reported sourly, "The target female is not aboard. Only the two pilots are inside."

Nick swore violently. "Where did they take her?"

The FBI man answered grimly, "I need you gentlemen to stay put a little longer while we have a quick…conversation…with these pilots."

It gave Nick grim satisfaction to know that it would be a very unpleasant conversation if the pilots didn't sing like canaries.

In about thirty seconds the FBI agent reported, "Smart boys. Decided to cooperate fully with us. They've given us the coordinates of a field where they dropped off your wife and her four captors. They said she called one of the men who grabbed her something like Kum-bay-ah."

"Moubayed," Nick said through gritted teeth. "I'll kill him with my bare hands if he's harmed a hair on her head."

"Yeah, well, let's find her first and take it from there," the FBI agent retorted with a grunt as he and most of his men sprinted for their helicopter. One agent was left behind to hold the pilots until police could arrive on the scene.

And then the FBI chopper and the SUVs were off again, speeding into the night.

* * *

"I regret to inform you, General, that I am going to be unable to accept your deal," Katy said quietly.

Sharaf exploded into curses on the other end of the phone. Thankfully most of it was in Arabic, and she'd never bothered to learn obscenities in that tongue.

"I'll kill you if you don't take the deal!" he bellowed.

"Some things are worth dying for, General. I learned that from my husband. Some principles are bigger than one man or one woman. He was willing to die for his country. If I am to be a worthy queen to him and to the Baraqi people—my people—then I have to be willing to make the same sacrifice."

It felt right. It was insane. Purely suicidal. But it was the only decision she could live—or die with—in peace.

She didn't ask to be thrown into the middle of this high-stakes political crisis, had only vaguely understood the implications when she'd agreed to Nick's request to have his baby. It had really been a matter of human compassion to ease a dying man's last days. And, of course, it hadn't hurt that the dying man was a charming, charismatic prince. But all this other bigger stuff—honor, duty and country—hadn't been part of what she understood to be the initial bargain at all.

Thanks to Nick, however, it appeared she'd grown into all three.

She waited out Sharaf's screaming. And when he paused to regain his breath, she said reasonably, "That money is Baraq's future. It's food and medicine for children. It's schools and jobs. It's a better future for thousands of people, men and women alike. How can I possibly give all that away just to save my own neck? It would be supremely selfish of me to take your deal. I can't and won't do it."

"You're dead!" he screamed. "Hand the phone to Moubayed."

Cold terror washed over her. *Steady, Katy.* Just because she'd made a decision that would probably cost her life, that didn't mean she was going to roll over and go down without a fight.

"Of course, General," she said smoothly, eyeing the ground at her feet. She spotted what she needed and sidled to her left a bit. And then she flung the phone down upon a rock and stomped on it all in one motion.

Moubayed lurched. "What the hell did you do that for?"

She shrugged with a casualness she didn't feel at all. "He and I had no more to say to each other."

Moubayed cursed at her long and hard in Arabic. As he threw his tantrum, he revealed more than he probably should have. As she'd hoped, she had him in a bit of a pickle. His impulse was to kill her, but he had strict orders from Sharaf not to hurt her. Until he got in touch with the general again, he didn't dare do anything.

And now it was time to keep him occupied and not borrowing one of his henchmen's phones to dial Sharaf back. She bolted.

She wasn't the greatest athlete the world had ever seen, but she had the element of surprise on her side and she had desperation to speed her steps. She darted into the woods and dodged between the trees, slipping into and through every narrow space she could find.

Moubayed and his men were all much bigger and huskier in build than her.

It was a relief to run for her life. Moving like this made her feel as though she had some small measure of control over her fate. Thankfully Moubayed and his men didn't pull out guns and start shooting. They were going to have to actually catch her and tackle her.

She heard them crashing through the woods. All four were swearing freely and calling back and forth to each other. *In Arabic.*

She paused to listen to them, crouching in the shadowed lee of a tree to catch her breath. They didn't know she could understand them.

The four men were setting up an ambush. Apparently there was some kind of barrier ahead—a riverbank maybe? She didn't know the word they were using. At any rate, they were content to herd Katy toward it and trap her.

She looked left and right. She had to hide. Let them move past her. And then she'd sneak back in the direction she'd come from. She spotted a heavy growth of weeds and shrubs a few yards away. If she could just get under that, maybe she'd be okay.

And maybe not. But it wasn't as if she had a whole lot of better options. The net was closing around her.

"We've got heat signatures on radar," one of the pilots announced over the general radio frequency everyone was listening in on.

"What kind of heat signatures?" Nick replied sharply.

"Human. Four, no five of them. In the woods below us. Four of them are on the move. The fifth one appears to be—" the guy paused for a second and then went on grimly "—prone on the ground."

Nick's heart dropped to his feet. They were too late. *Dear God, take my life in return for hers.* After everything they'd been through together, after how close they'd gotten to having it all, they couldn't fail now.

The driver said off-radio, "The helicopter will put men out on ropes. They'll rappel in as close to the action as they can. We're going to have to park in the nearest field and hoof it in on foot."

Nick went totally numb. He felt nothing. Saw nothing. Heard nothing. She *had* to be alive. He'd die if something had happened to her.

Katy plastered herself flat against the cold, wet ground under the bush and barely dared to breathe. She covered herself up with leaves as best she could, but she dared not disturb the forest floor too much or that in itself would give her away.

Moubayed was just drawing even with her, passing off to her right at a distance of no more than twenty feet. He was moving slowly, stealthily, like a hunter tracking its prey. She watched him through eyes barely slitted open. Another slow, light, *careful* inhalation on her part.

He took another step.

She held her breath until her lungs were on fire. And then exhaled by agonizing degrees. She felt as if she was going to pass out before she allowed herself to inhale again, a welcome relief to her pain.

Another couple steps by Moubayed.

A few more, and she'd be out of his primary line of

sight. She drew in another breath, slightly more easily than last time. Her plan might just work after all.

And then all hell broke loose. Something incredibly loud swooped in overhead, and dark objects came crashing down through the trees all at once. Moubayed whirled and began firing a gun he'd pulled out of somewhere on his person, and shots rang out in return. All of Moubayed's men were firing now, and the dark falling objects turned out to be men shouting back and forth at each other and roaring for Moubayed and his men to surrender or die.

She buried her face in the dirt and prayed like crazy that this new threat wouldn't kill her. She'd been so close to getting away. So close to safety. To making her way back to Nick and their love and happily ever after. It would be too ironic if she died now after all they'd gone through together trying to keep Nick alive.

The firefight was pure chaos. She plastered herself even flatter against the ground and prayed with all her might that a stray bullet wouldn't hit her—or worse, that Moubayed didn't turn his weapon on her and take her out in the midst of the shoot-out.

But she wasn't so lucky.

When the lead slammed into her, she was more aware of the impact of it than the pain. Time slowed, and her thoughts became crystal clear, each one outlined in bright light. The bullet had hit right where her neck and shoulder joined. She felt a gush of warm wetness. She was bleeding then. She pressed her left hand against the wound. But it was futile. Blood seeped unchecked over and through her fingers.

The firefight went on around her for a lifetime after that. Long enough for her to remember the first time she'd seen Nick, so battered and yet so beautiful. Her shock the moment he'd told her who he was. That unforgettable moment when he'd asked her to have his baby. Their unorthodox wedding. And then her thoughts slowed until time stopped altogether as each beautiful, tender, heartrending moment of their lovemaking passed through her mind's eye.

She smiled against the wet leaves and mud as she felt consciousness slipping away from her. It had been a good life. They'd loved deeply and well. And silently she mouthed the same promise to Nick that he'd made to her the last time she'd seen him in Baraq.

She would be his for all eternity. She bade him to live joyfully and love well. And when his days were passed, she would be waiting for him at heaven's gate.

Her lips stilled. She felt cold. And then it all faded away to silence and dark, leaving behind only peace. And warmth. And love.

Chapter 16

Nick heard the gunshots even before he was out of the vehicle. And sensation came flooding back—a chilling rush of panic. He had to find Katy!

More gunfire erupted, a spate of it rattling through the trees in front of him. He put on an extra burst of speed. Surely Katy wasn't caught in the middle of that! It sounded worse than the night the coup took place.

He crashed through the trees without a care for himself. He was only vaguely aware of branches slashing at him, of cuts opening up on his face and hands. He had to find her. He *had* to.

"Katy!" he called into the din of voices shouting all around.

She didn't answer. But he probably couldn't have heard her if she did.

The shooting began to slow down, and he drew close to the epicenter of the fight. He began to see shapes ahead. Armed men wearing night-vision goggles, kneeling in combat shooting positions, brandishing lethal weapons.

"Katy!" he shouted again. This time he could actually hear his own voice.

Still no answer.

And then a male voice called out from in front of him and to the left. "Subject located and down. She's shot. Bleeding and unresponsive."

Nick's world ended right there. He sprinted for all he was worth toward the sound of the man's voice. And fell to the ground beside a pile of brush that two of the men had hastily yanked aside. Beside his Katy.

Even in this near-total blackness, her skin was pale. Unnaturally so. And a pool of liquid black spread under her right shoulder.

He was too incoherent to form words of prayer. He just sent his desperation and love toward heaven and hoped that whatever deity who heard it understood.

One of the FBI agents shouldered his way through the others. He knelt quickly and put his hands on Katy's neck, looking for a pulse.

And then he announced, "I've got a pulse. Regular but thready. Have the chopper drop the crash kit."

Someone barked tersely into a radio while the medic used a flashlight to find the source of the blood. It didn't take long. A ragged wound across the top of her shoulder near the base of her neck.

The medic grabbed a paper packet and ripped it

open with his teeth. He pressed a large gauze pad hard against the wound. "She's bleeding freely, but the bullet didn't penetrate her shoulder. It just ripped across the surface. Assuming she hasn't lost a lot of blood, she should be okay. But I still want to get her to a hospital ASAP. Someone get a cuff on her and monitor her blood pressure."

The weight lifted off Nick's chest a little. He still wasn't going to be satisfied until she looked up at him and smiled. Until a doctor declared her completely well.

"Has the chopper got a basket?" the medic called out.

"Affirmative," someone answered.

"Drop it. We've got to get this patient out of here. Her blood pressure's dropping."

After that, it all passed in a blur. A metal mesh basket was dropped through the trees. Katy was gently lifted into it. The medic climbed in beside her. And then she disappeared into the night. It reminded Nick eerily of watching her ascend to heaven.

A bunch of men crashed through the trees to announce that all four tangos were dead. Whatever the hell a tango was. Obviously they weren't referring to a dance. Nick could only hope they were referring to Moubayed and his men.

He raced out of the woods with Travis and a few of the FBI men to the SUVs. Nick barely registered the frantic ride back to Bethesda, Maryland, and the naval hospital there. A blur of white corridors and bright lights, and then an interminable wait pacing in a waiting room with vinyl upholstered chairs and a television that wouldn't shut up.

And then a doctor came to the door in green surgical scrubs. "Mr. Ramsey?"

He whirled, searching the man's face for a hint of whether it was good or bad news. "Yes? How is she?"

"She's going to be fine. She lost a lot of blood, but we have her stabilized and the bleeding stopped. The bullet grazed an artery in her shoulder. Had help not gotten to her as quickly as it did…" He didn't finish the sentence. He didn't have to.

"And the baby?"

The doctor nodded. "Fine. We'll continue to monitor your wife closely for the next few days and make sure there are no complications to her or the baby."

Nick's legs suddenly wouldn't support his weight. He collapsed into a chair and put his hands over his face. What had he done in his lifetime to earn having his prayers for Katy answered, he didn't know. But he wasn't about to question the wisdom of whatever higher being had blessed him so.

He heard an unsteady breath beside him and realized Travis had collapsed in the seat next to his.

Nick pulled himself together enough to ask, "Can I see her?"

"Yes. She's lightly sedated and resting, but you can sit with her if you like."

Katy swam slowly through the fog surrounding her. Time passed. She woke up again. She was still groggy. Still surrounded in fog. But she was aware of sheets over her and bandages tight upon her shoulder, which throbbed.

More time passed.

The second time she woke up, she fully awoke.

Nick was there. Right beside her. "Hi, beautiful," he murmured.

"Hi," she whispered, surprised that was all the sound that came out of her throat.

"Don't try to talk."

Her hand fluttered weakly toward her abdomen.

Nick captured her fingers and smiled reassuringly. "The baby's fine."

She sagged against the mattress. Thank God. She became aware of other people in the room. Her parents. And Travis. And…

She frowned. The woman who'd served her tea in Akuba? Was she hallucinating, then?

"Am I awake?" she mumbled.

Nick squeezed her hand gently. "You've been asleep for several hours. They had to do a little surgery to repair an artery in your shoulder. But everything's fine now."

Good. That was good. She nodded her head. She felt so weak and woozy. "Who's that lady?"

Nick glanced over his shoulder. "My mother. When she heard that Moubayed shot you, she insisted on coming here to be with us. I never realized the woman you met in Baraq was my mother."

Katy tried to shrug, but piercing pain in her shoulder stopped that idea cold. "She never told me her name," Katy whispered.

"She was in grave danger. Had Sharaf spotted her, she'd have been arrested and likely killed, too. It was crazy of her to risk her life like that." He tossed an I'll-talk-to-you-later glare at the woman, and his mother's chin lifted defiantly.

Katy's free hand settled on her abdomen. Smiling at Nick's mother, she murmured, "It's a mommy thing. Wild horses couldn't have dragged her away from you when you were in trouble. Don't blame her."

Nick sighed. "At any rate, she's delighted we got married. She liked you a lot, apparently." He rolled his eyes and added under his breath, "Your mother and mine have been gushing nonstop over having a grandchild ever since they found out you were going to be okay."

A dark stubble covered his cheeks and chin, and his hair was disheveled. But then he smiled at her, and she'd never seen him look more gorgeous.

She was feeling stronger by the minute. The anesthesia was wearing off quickly now. She spoke again, and this time her voice worked reasonably well. "I talked to Sharaf."

Nick lurched to his feet. "What in the hell did he want?"

"He wanted me to give him all the money. In return, he promised to let us live and to name our first child heir to the Baraqi throne."

Nick sucked in a quick breath between his teeth. "Did you take the deal?"

"No."

Nick stared. "Why ever not? It's everything we could have asked for and more! We'd live out our lives together in safety—" he squeezed her fingers "—and the Ramsey legacy would not be completely broken. When I thought I'd lost you earlier, I realized I don't care a bit about being king. Not without you to share it with."

She smiled weakly. "I said no because I realized I am a queen. Responsible for my people. Our people. And they need that money. It would take years, if ever, for Baraq to amass that much wealth again. They need it if Baraq is to lift itself into the twenty-first century."

Nick stared at her. Stared some more.

And then he laughed. Long and loud. Finally he announced in high humor, "Never in my entire life did I expect to hear a line like that come out of your mouth. Here you are deciding that kingdom and country are all-important just when I'm finally deciding family and home are all-important."

She smiled back at him. It was ironic, indeed. But then she coughed, gasping in pain as her shoulder jostled.

Nick jumped forward in concern. "I'll go get the doctor. They can give you painkillers to make you comfortable."

She grasped his hand more strongly to keep him from pulling away from her. Startled, he turned back to her.

"I'll handle the pain. It helps me know I'm alive. Besides, with the baby, I shouldn't take too many strong medications."

Nick subsided onto the stool beside the bed, smiling at her.

She said, "Tell me about the rest of your press release. Sharaf told me you'd put one out to announce the transfer of Baraq's entire treasury to me."

"I hoped it would force Sharaf not to kill you."

"It worked. He ordered Moubayed not to harm me."

Nick's fingers squeezed hers. "Travis and I had a press conference scheduled with you and me and an

Undersecretary of State from your government to announce a deal between us to take my throne back from Sharaf."

"How did the press conference go?"

He shrugged. "I canceled it. When we got the word you'd been kidnapped, I skipped out and came after you."

"Oh, Nick," she cried softly. "Was the State Department man angry?"

"He was annoyed."

"Did he back out of the deal?"

"Not in so many words. He expressed concern for your welfare and fed me platitudes about family coming first. But Travis is worried that we blew our chance to push him into action against Sharaf." He added, "Don't worry about it. It doesn't matter. All I care about is that you and the baby are safe."

"Yes, but it was such a golden opportunity to get your country back."

He laid a gentle finger on her lips to silence her. "I'm serious. My throne would be meaningless without you beside me to share it."

Katy stared at him, stunned. "You really mean that?"

"Of course."

"Come here so I can kiss you, you wonderful man."

He complied, his mouth touching hers gently. The walls fell away and it was all back in a flash—every bit of light and heat and soaring beauty they'd ever made between them.

And then a throat cleared behind them. Nick lifted his mouth away from hers, and reluctantly she let him go.

It was Travis.

"What do you want?" she said irritably. "You interrupted us at the good part."

He laughed and stepped into the room. "I thought you two might like to see this."

It was a faxed copy of a letter written in Arabic on royal Baraqi letterhead. Nick read it aloud in English.

"'I, General Hamzad Sharaf, do hereby relinquish all control and governance of Baraq and do return sovereignty in full to His Royal Highness, Nikolas Ramsey, and his queen, Katrina McMann-Ramsey—'"

Nick looked up, his eyes glowing as fiercely golden as a lion's. "When did you get this?" he demanded.

Travis grinned. "About five minutes ago. You wouldn't happen to know anything about it, would you?"

Nick colored slightly. "I asked Kareem and George to have a chat with Sharaf a little while ago. They described to him in detail what being a prisoner was like. And apparently, they speculated on what Baraqi and international opinion would make of a man who kidnapped and threatened to kill an innocent pregnant woman and whose men actually did shoot her. He swore up and down he had nothing to do with Moubayed's actions."

"I heard Moubayed talking to Sharaf on the phone. Sharaf knew full well what Moubayed was up to. He's lying!" Katy exclaimed and then winced in pain. She subsided against the pillows and said more quietly, "Sharaf told me he'd have me killed when I refused his deal. Screamed it at me, in fact. Then he told me to give the phone back to Moubayed. I threw the cell phone on the ground and stomped on it. I didn't want Moubayed to get the order."

Nick nodded. "The FBI surmised as much when they found the remains of the phone."

Travis interjected, "You'll need to make a formal statement to that effect, sis. The FBI will need it to close its case on Moubayed."

She nodded and Nick continued, "They were able to recover data from Moubayed's cell phone memory chip and found Sharaf's private phone number in it. They also found a record of a call being placed from Moubayed's phone to Sharaf a few minutes before the shootout. Not that it matters to Moubayed anymore. He's dead."

Katy was relieved that the man would never try to harm her or the baby again.

Nick shrugged. "At any rate, Sharaf decided a quiet retirement was preferable to a public execution."

Katy looked up at Nick, her heart shining in her eyes. "Could it be more perfect? We've got our country back, the baby's safe and, best of all, we have each other."

He gazed down at her, infinite love mirrored in his eyes, as well. "It looks like you got your happily ever after, and I found my very own Cinderella. Remind me to have a pair of glass slippers made for you. And a carriage in the shape of a pumpkin."

Katy laughed—and winced. "Thanks, but all I need is Prince Charming."

"I am yours, heart and soul. For all eternity."

She reflected that, for an anonymous humanitarian relief worker of no special note, she hadn't done half-bad in the fairy-tale-ending department—a charming prince, an enchanted palace and, most importantly of all, true love.

She had, indeed, found her very own happily ever after.

They both had.

* * * * *

BRIDES OF PENHALLY BAY

Medical™ is proud to welcome you to Penhally Bay Surgery where you can meet the team led by caring and commanding Dr Nick Tremayne. For the next twelve months we will bring you an emotional, tempting romance – devoted doctors, single fathers, a sheikh surgeon, royalty, blushing brides and miracle babies will warm your heart…

Let us whisk you away to this Cornish coastal town – to a place where hearts are made whole.

Turn the page for a sneak preview from *Christmas Eve Baby* by Caroline Anderson – the first book in the BRIDES OF PENHALLY BAY series.

CHRSTMAS EVE BABY

by

Caroline Anderson

Ben crossed the room, standing by the window, looking out. It was a pleasant room, and from the window he could see across the boatyard to the lifeboat station and beyond it the sea.

He didn't notice, though, not really. Didn't take it in, couldn't have described the colour of the walls or the furniture, because there was only one thing he'd really seen, only one thing he'd been aware of since Lucy had got out of her car.

Lucy met his eyes, but only with a huge effort, and he could see the emotions racing through their wary, soft brown depths. God only knows what his own expression was, but he held her gaze for a long moment before she coloured and looked away.

'Um–can I make you some tea?' she offered, and he gave a short, disbelieving cough of laughter.

'Don't you think there's something we should talk about first?' he suggested, and she hesitated, her hand on the kettle, catching her lip between those neat, even teeth and nibbling it unconsciously.

'I intend to,' she began, and he laughed and propped his hips on the edge of the desk, his hands each side gripping the thick, solid wood as if his life depended on it.

'When, exactly? Assuming, as I am, perhaps a little rashly, that unless that's a beachball you've got up your jumper it has something to do with me?'

She put the kettle down with a little thump and turned towards him, her eyes flashing fire. 'Rashly? *Rashly?* Is that what you think of me? That I'd sleep with you and then go and fall into bed with another man?'

He shrugged, ignoring the crazy, irrational flicker of hope that it was, indeed, his child. 'I don't know. I would hope not, but I don't know anything about your private life. Not any more,' he added with a tinge of regret.

'Well, you should know enough about me to know that isn't the way I do things.'

'So how do you do things, Lucy?' he asked, trying to stop the anger from creeping into his voice. 'Like your father? You don't like it, so you just pretend it hasn't happened?'

'And what was I supposed to do?' she asked, her eyes flashing sparks again. 'We weren't seeing each other. We'd agreed.'

'But this, surely, changes things? Or should have. Unless you just weren't going to tell me? It must have made it simpler for you.'

She turned away again, but not before he saw her eyes fill, and guilt gnawed at him. 'Simpler?'

she said. 'That's not how I'd describe it.'

'So why not tell me, then?' he said, his voice softening. 'Why, in all these months, didn't you tell me that I'm going to be a father?'

'I was going to,' she said, her voice little more than a whisper. 'But after everything – I didn't know how to. It's just all so difficult – '

'But it *is* mine.'

She nodded, her hair falling over her face and obscuring it from him. 'Yes. Yes, it's yours.'

His heart soared, and for a ridiculous moment he felt like punching the air, but then he pulled himself together. Plenty of time for that later, once he'd got all the facts. Down to the nitty-gritty, he thought, and asked the question that came to the top of the heap.

'Does your father know it's mine…?'

She shook her head, and he winced.

'Have you had lunch?' she said suddenly.

'Lunch?' he said, his tone disbelieving. 'No. I got held up in Resus. There wasn't time.'

'Fancy coming back to my house and having something to eat? Only I'm starving, and I'm trying to eat properly, and biscuits and cakes and rubbish like that just won't cut the mustard.'

'Sounds good,' he said, not in the least bit hungry but desperate to be away from there and somewhere private while he assimilated this stunning bit of news.

She opened the door, grabbed her coat out of the staff room as they passed it and led him down the stairs.

They walked to her flat, along Harbour Road and up Bridge Street, the road that ran alongside the river and up out of the old town towards St Piran, the road he'd come in on. It was over a gift shop, in a steep little terrace typical of Cornish coastal towns and villages, and he wondered how she'd manage when she'd had the baby.

Not here, was the answer, especially when she led him through a door into a narrow little hallway and up the precipitous stairs to her flat. 'Make yourself at home, I'll find some food,' she said, a little breathless after her climb, and left him in the small living room. If he got close to the window he could see the sea, but apart from that it had no real charm. It was homely, though, and comfortable, and he wandered round it, picking up things and putting them down, measuring her life.

A book on pregnancy, a mother-and-baby magazine, a book of names, lying in a neat pile on the end of an old leather trunk in front of the sofa. More books in a bookcase, a cosy fleece blanket draped over the arm of the sofa, some flowers in a vase lending a little cheer.

He could see her through the kitchen door, pottering about and making sandwiches, and he went and propped himself in the doorway and watched her.

'I'd offer to help, but the room's too small for three of us,' he murmured, and she gave him a slightly nervous smile.

Why nervous? he wondered, and then realised that of course she was nervous. She had no idea what his attitude would be, whether he'd be pleased or angry, if he'd want to be involved in his child's life – any of it.

When he'd worked it out himself, he'd tell her. The only thing he did know, absolutely with total certainty, was that if, as she had said, this baby was his, he was going to be a part of its life for ever.

And that was non-negotiable.

* * * *